THE BLOOD ALLIANCE

International law supersedes all national governance and will be maintained by the Blood Alliance—a global council of equal parts lycan and vampire.

All resources are to be distributed evenly between lycan and vampire, including territory and blood. Societal standing and wealth, however, will be at the discretion of the individual packs and houses.

To kill, harm, or provoke a superior being is punishable by immediate death. All disputes must be presented to the Blood Alliance for final judgment.

Sexual relationships between lycans and vampires are strictly prohibited. However, business partnerships, where fruitful and appropriate, are permitted.

Humans are hereby classified as property and do not carry any legal rights. Each will be tagged through a sorting system based on merit, intelligence, bloodline, ability, and beauty. Prioritization to be established at birth and finalized on Blood Day.

Twelve mortals per year will be selected to compete for immortal blood status at the discretion of the Blood Alliance. From these twelve, two will be bitten by immortality. The others will die. To create a lycan or vampire outside of this process is unlawful and punishable by immediate death.

All other laws are at the discretion of the packs and royals but must not defy the Blood Alliance.

"Lily." Master Cedric's voice held a strange note to it. Not chilling or cruel like usual. But an odd deepness that made me warm all over. Except I didn't understand his comment. He seemed to always be talking about flowers.

And fighting.

And death.

And failing me.

I tried to shake my head, but that only made my dizziness worse.

"When was the last time you ate something?" he asked.

"Breakfast bag," I replied, my voice a bit hoarse.

He sighed. "And you've already missed dinner."

"Did I miss it again?" I wondered out loud, uncertain of the time. *Probably*, I thought. The window for picking up food was very strict, and he'd likely kept me too long for tonight's session.

His scent slithered around me as he pressed another kiss to my pulse. "So delicate and fragile," he whispered. "My sweet Lily flower."

My lips nearly curled down, but I caught the instinct at the last moment before I could react.

Reactions weren't allowed.

Humans who screamed—*died*.

Humans who showed displeasure—*died*.

Humans who displayed anything other than contentment or boredom—*died*.

My stomach rumbled then, stirring another wave of dizziness. He'd told me to get dressed and leave, but I couldn't move with his arm trapping me against him.

He slowly led me to the chair behind his desk. It was the only furniture in the room aside from the mats. "Sit," he said, his tone oddly soft.

LEXI C. FOSS

BLOOD
DAY

WELCOME TO BLOOD UNIVERSITY.
GRADUATION IS DEATH.

Blood Day: Part One

Editing by: Outthink Editing, LLC

Proofreading by: Katie Schmahl

Cover Design: Covers by Julie

Cover Photography: CJC Photography

Cover Models: Eric Guilmette & Skyler Simpson

Title Page Design: Covers by Sanja

Published by: Ninja Newt Publishing, LLC

eBook Edition

ISBN: 978-1-68530-174-3

Paperback Edition

ISBN: 978-1-68530-175-0

❀ Created with Vellum

USA TODAY BESTSELLING AUTHOR
LEXI C. FOSS
BLOOD DAY

WELCOME TO BLOOD UNIVERSITY.
GRADUATION IS DEATH.

BLOOD DAY

PART I

Blood Day.
The deadly graduation ceremony that dictates who I will
become in this world run by vampires and lycans.

There is no escape. Nowhere to run. Obey or die.

My name isn't relevant. My identity fails to mean a thing.
It's my scores that count. And Master Cedric is hell-bent
on failing me.

I bow. I beg. I crawl.
But nothing is good enough for the ancient vampire with
cruel dark eyes. He wants me to bleed exclusively for him.
Yet that's not how this society works.

I can't fail. My life depends on it.
I will fight until my last breath. Even if that means dying
on my knees before the vampire god who rules my
classroom.

Welcome to the future where the superior bloodlines make the rules.
You're about to enter the Blood University world, where humans have
no rights. No choices. And there are no second chances.
Proceed at your own risk.

WARNING NOTE

You're about to enter the world of the Blood University, where humans are groomed and prepared for their eventual fate in the Blood Alliance world.

It's dark dystopian depravity. It's gritty. It's cruel. And it may make some readers uncomfortable.

Humans have no rights in this world. Vampires and lycans rule, humans are their cattle, and the relationships formed between them are forbidden, harsh, and often vicious. Power exchange is very real here. Submission is required. And biting is considered an endearment, even when it results in death.

Enter if you dare.
Run if you must.

Once upon a time, humankind ruled the world while lycans and
vampires lived in secret.
This is no longer that time.
Welcome to the future where the superior bloodlines make the rules.
Proceed at your own risk.

THE BLOOD UNIVERSITY

Humans are to be relegated to the Blood University system at birth. They will be trained, tested, and prepared for their eventual place in society.

Course studies will include basics in standard education, defensive training, obedience, Blood Alliance politics, sexual studies, and general lessons in servitude.

An equal number of vampires and lycans will serve as professors to train in these various areas. These valued Masters are collectively known as the Blood University Council. They are the superiors and report only to the Magistrate.

All mortals are to be prepared to face their fate on Blood Day—a formal occasion that occurs annually where humans of twenty-two years of age are assigned to their permanent positions within society.

Weak genetics serve no purpose in this world. Those who do not measure up to societal standards will be removed at the discretion of the Blood University Council.

Failure to comply is death.
Failure to obey is death.
Failure to perform is death.

Enrollment is mandatory.
There are no alternative paths.
Humans conform or die.

BLOOD
DAY
PART I

PROLOGUE
CEDRIC

I covet something that isn't mine. A human. Property of the Blood Alliance. Someone who will likely be dead by this time next year, if not sooner.

But I can't help it.

Every time I lay eyes on her, my blood simmers to a boil. I *want* her. It's her eyes, those blue-green irises that swirl with a soul I long to devour.

She tries so hard to please me.

I fail her each time.

It's wrong. However, the higher her marks, the more likely another will notice her. And I refuse to let that happen. I'm protecting her from a worse fate. Or that's how I justify it, anyway.

In reality, I'm damning her. Ensuring she'll perish before I ever have a chance to know her. It kills me to do it. Yet I can't afford the temptation. She needs to be removed. Permanently.

I'll admire her from afar.

Degrade her up close.

And secretly smile as she begs for my remorse.

This is a cruel world filled with harsh choices. I choose to let her die. Even if a part of me will expire with her.

My soul. My heart. The last shreds of my humanity.

Good riddance. There's no place in this reality for such frivolities.

This is the era of the Blood Alliance. A world maintained by the superior bloodlines—my vampire brethren and the lycans.

Mortals are only here to serve.

And she'll serve me by dying.

My Lily.

Oh, that's not her real name. It's what I choose to call her with that creamy complexion and those soft, stem-like irises.

She's blossomed for the last time.

I'll pick apart her petals. Watch her wilt. Then bury her with the rest of my hope.

This existence is not what it used to be.

No love. No life. No light.

Goodbye, my sweet little flower. May you bloom again in the afterlife.

LILY

ANOTHER FAILURE. HOW IS THIS EVEN POSSIBLE?

I did everything right on this exam. Every movement. Every kick. Every punch. Yet, Master Cedric failed me. *Again*.

My teeth ground together, and my fingers threatened to curl into fists against the paper in my hand. At this rate, I would absolutely fail his class. Which meant the Immortal Cup was out of the question for my future.

Only the best and highest-marked students qualified to compete for immortality.

I wouldn't even come close with these marks against my record.

I just wished I knew what I'd done wrong. How to please him. How to fix my technique to his satisfaction. Everyone else seemed to understand except me.

I'd practiced day and night.

And I swore my angles had been just right.

Maybe taking a fighting course had been a bad idea. But becoming a Vigil was my second choice to immortality. At least Vigils had a semblance of rights in this world. Unlike practically every other designation.

I excelled in every other course.

So why not this one?

I bit my lip as I considered the vampire in question who continued to fail me. He stood at the front of the room in a pair of black slacks and a white button-down shirt. It was what he always wore, even while demonstrating fighting moves on the mat.

Elegance personified.

Gorgeous, too.

Midnight eyes. A square chin shadowed by a neatly trimmed beard that framed his handsome jaw. Full lips. Thick brown hair that was tousled near his ears. And a body that reminded me of a sleek wolf more than a vampire, his fluid-like grace something that drew my gaze to him every time he moved.

"Is there something you need, Prospect Four Hundred and Seven, Year One Hundred Seventeen?" Master Cedric asked, his deep tones sending a chill down my spine.

Because that was me—*Prospect Four Hundred and Seven, Year One Hundred Seventeen.*

We were all named by our prospect numbers and the year we would be assigned to our fates.

This was year one hundred sixteen.

Which made me almost finished with my training.

Assuming I didn't fail this course.

Master Cedric's dark gaze lifted to mine, the cruelty lurking in the depths of his irises causing me to freeze before him. The glimmer of irritation in his irises was impossible to miss, as was the curl of his lip as he glared at me in obvious impatience.

Because he'd asked me something.

Something I could no longer remember.

Not with him staring me down as though I were his next meal.

An accurate assessment, given my mortal status and his superiority over humankind.

I lowered my gaze, demonstrating my weaker stance and bestowing unto him the respect due for his position.

Except my focus dropped to the paper in my hand, reminding me that this vampire had just failed me—*again*—and I didn't understand why. I wanted to improve my skills not just for him but for myself, too. Because I knew I could excel at being a Vigil if given the appropriate marks.

"Master Cedric," I began, swallowing as I tried to form my words. "Are there, um, any opportunities or courses you recommend for me to improve my skills? I feel like I missed a class before yours, and I want to perfect my technique to more adequately meet your expectations."

Even though I'm reasonably certain I've done everything right thus far.

But clearly, I'm missing something.

So help me. Please.

Those last few statements were thoughts I wouldn't dare utter in his presence. It was a miracle I could even voice the request for help. Vampires and lycans weren't known for their kindness or acceptance of failure. When a mortal proved to be unworthy, the human became food.

I didn't want to become food.

Just the notion of it left me feeling cold and uncertain. Or perhaps it was Master Cedric's chilling silence that stirred the hairs along the back of my neck.

I risked a glance upward, the impulse one I knew better than to allow, and froze beneath his narrowed stare. Obsidian flames danced around his pupils, the superiority and power pouring off him in an intoxicating wave that threatened to suffocate my very being.

"I'm sorry," I whispered, immediately kneeling before him. "I don't mean to continue to fail you."

I'm going to die here. Today. In this classroom. Because—

His palm went to the top of my head, sending a mixture of ice and warmth through my veins. That single touch spread fire across my skin, making me acutely aware of his dominance. Not just from being a vampire, or even a man, but simply from being *him.*

He was graceful and meticulous, and chillingly concise in class.

And he was *touching* me.

Not harshly. Just petting me softly as though I were a disobedient animal kneeling at his feet.

An animal he intended to punish.

Kill.

Maybe even fuck.

I stopped breathing, that final thought making my thighs clench. I'd witnessed vampires taking their prey hundreds of times.

Humans were naturally drawn to them, inherently submissive, and many screamed in ecstasy even as they died.

Would Master Cedric do that to me now? Thread his fingers through my hair, drag me to his desk, and take me against the hard wood while drinking me dry?

It would be so easy for him. No one would ask any questions. No one would reprimand him. I resembled prey in a university run by predators.

This place was meant to weed out the weak, to ensure only the strongest of mortals would survive.

My marks until now were exemplary.

But I'd made a mistake taking Master Cedric's course.

And now I would pay for that mistake with my life.

The constant thrumming in my head made me dizzy, my body begging me to breathe. To move. To do something other than kneel here at Master Cedric's feet.

I swallowed, my eyes falling shut, resignation steeling my nerves.

Some humans fought in their final moments. Others went down gracefully.

Predators enjoyed the fight, that moment where their victims attempted to flee, to scream, to beg for mercy. Something told me Master Cedric would be no different.

All I wanted was to improve my marks.

To prove my worth.

To potentially become something *more*.

But this vampire had loathed me from the moment he'd laid eyes on me.

And I'd possessed the audacity to question him.

"You're such a delicate little flower," Master Cedric mused, his fingers drawing through the strands of my hair and interrupting me from my inner torment. "So pretty and meek."

It's what I'm meant to be, I wanted to reply. But I knew better than to speak. I'd already tested his patience by being bold enough to request help.

A stupid, naïve move.

Why had I stayed after class? What had given me the nerve to speak to him?

Shock, maybe.

Because I couldn't believe he'd failed me *again*. After all my training and accurate movements, he'd told me it was all wrong. He'd called me *weak*.

Your left leg is too bent.

Your foot is off-center when you kick.

You missed your target by several inches.

I'd read that feedback five times, confused by each word. I'd just kept thinking, *He's wrong. This is all wrong.* Then my mind had wandered to the Immortal Cup and the very real impact these marks would have on my future, and I'd forgotten myself completely.

I'd remained when everyone else had left.

Leaving me alone with a predator.

A predator who *hated* me.

And now I was on my knees, awaiting his punishment.

Because there was no mistaking the situation here—he would punish me for acting out of line. I'd questioned him. Asked for direction. He wasn't my mentor. That wasn't how this world worked.

I survived by keeping my head down and following directions.

To request assistance was *not* obedient. It suggested I felt he owed me an explanation. No superior owed any human an explanation for their choices and decisions.

Kneel.

Worship.

Admire.

Those were the core rules for my kind.

Along with a myriad of others about serving our Masters and doing whatever they commanded of us.

His thumb drew a line along my jaw to my chin, capturing it with ease and guiding my focus upward. "It's bold to request my assistance, little flower."

I swallowed. "I'm sorry."

"Are you?" He cocked his head. "Or are you merely terrified of my reaction to your request?"

I blinked. "Both." It came out in a whisper, my admission causing his eyebrows to lift.

"A truth," he replied, his eyes roaming over my features. "I suppose that shouldn't surprise me. It's one of your more positive traits." His intense gaze fell to my lips. "As is your mouth."

The dark meaning in his words wasn't lost on me.

I'd taken two sexual arts courses on how to properly please males—both lycans and vampires. All humans chose a preferred skill in that realm of existence, and I'd opted for oral studies. I still had one more class to pick, and I hadn't decided yet what it would be.

They were important marks for our overall record.

Because many of us would be sent to the breeding camps.

Others would be drafted for royal harems.

I wanted neither of those fates.

However, the way he'd remarked on my mouth suggested it was my destiny anyway. Because it meant he'd taken note of my marks in those areas.

Perhaps that was why he chose to fail me in his course —he didn't see me as worthy of being a Vigil.

My jaw clenched in response, my reaction innate.

And entirely wrong.

Because he caught it.

His eyes narrowed, indicating that he read my response as open defiance.

"I want to do better," I blurted out, wanting to explain myself to him. "I... I'm trying..."

His eyebrows rose. "Am I supposed to care?"

"No," I answered quickly. "I'm aware that I'm... that this isn't..." I couldn't finish, his intense stare silencing me from speaking. His dark gaze reminded me of a stormy night, the black orbs glistening with unshed lightning as he waited to strike.

I should have just apologized.

No, I should never have stayed. I should have accepted my failure and left.

Because now I was going to die.

And I doubted he would make it pleasurable.

"You want to learn how to please me, little flower?" he

asked, and there was something in his tone that stirred a flutter in my abdomen. A hint of promise that captivated my entire focus.

"Yes, Master Cedric," I told him. "I do." It was the truth. I'd been trying to figure out how to appease him for months.

His lips curled ever so slightly at the edges, causing my heart to skip a beat.

Beautiful.

All predators were.

But something about him and his features called to me more than anyone or anything else. Perhaps because this was the longest I'd ever been allowed to observe one of his kind. He still had my chin clasped between his forefinger and thumb, forcing me to hold his alluring gaze.

It was a dangerous game.

One he'd started with his touch.

Or maybe he felt I'd initiated it with my boldness.

Regardless, I was utterly enthralled, waiting for him to speak, to deliver my fate.

His touch softened, his thumb tracing my jaw once more as he slid his fingers back into my hair to grab a fistful of my strands.

I didn't react, allowing him to manhandle me as he saw fit, and that only seemed to amuse him more.

"Watching you fail pleases me," he said softly, his gaze holding a touch of some hidden emotion I couldn't define. "You're like a pretty wilting flower, trying so hard to bloom beneath the midnight sun." His grip tightened in my hair, his gaze narrowing. "Death suits you, darling. Perhaps you should embrace it."

CEDRIC

THOSE DAMN IRISES WERE HYPNOTIZING ME, MAKING ME want to do something forbidden. *Keep her. Tame her. Make her mine.*

She looked so fucking tempting on her knees, her pretty, sad eyes staring up at me in clear shock.

I'd just admitted to failing her on purpose because it *pleased* me.

And she had no idea what to say. How to react. Yet I could almost taste the part of her that wanted to rebel, to fight my decision and demand an explanation.

But like a good little human, she kept her exquisite mouth shut.

Because she wasn't allowed to question her superiors.

Maybe she would flourish after all. Bow down and beg. Suck some royal cock for the next decade or so until she lost that life in her eyes.

Which was precisely what I didn't want to see happen.

She was too beautiful, too inspiring, too lovely for such a fate.

And yet her eyes took on a glimmer of that look now as she stared up at me, her mind processing my words.

I watched each emotion flutter through those alluring irises—first shock, then bleak acceptance, and finally a hint of fiery resolve.

Oh, yes, more, I thought, chasing that emotion across her features and loving the way it lit a fire in her cheeks.

She wanted to prove me wrong.

To fight.

To find a way around the failures in my course and pursue her dreams.

There was just one detail she failed to understand. "When you fail my course, you won't be eligible for future combat classes," I told her. "So maybe you'll focus on sexual arts instead." My gaze went to her mouth for what felt like the hundredth time. Her lips were perfect, fuckable, *full.* Just like her tits. "If you're lucky, they'll send you to a harem," I continued. "If you're not, you'll end up in a breeding camp, or worse."

True words.

Harsh words.

But she needed to understand her fate.

I was doing her a service by failing her, by degrading her scores to a point where no one would notice. Because most harems were worse than the breeding camps.

"They play dangerous games," I warned her, my voice lowering to a whisper. "Dangerous games meant to break the spirits of those desiring favoritism. You'll be lucky to survive initiation." I relinquished my hold on her hair, my fingers itching to run through her silky strands.

So soft.

So light.

So opposite of my traits.

Speaking freely to an inferior being was frowned upon by my kind. I wouldn't be punished for it, of course. But she would. If anyone heard the words I'd just said to her, she would die. Perhaps by my hand.

They'd give me the option, something that some might assume to be a punishment.

However, superior beings didn't feel for their pets.

Making it a rather bland assumption indeed.

No, it'd be more of an offer than a form of castigation. They'd ask if I wanted to enjoy her as a snack first, which I would.

Then I'd take her to her grave.

Peacefully.

Beautifully.

Passionately.

My gift to her. And a memory to haunt me for a lifetime.

Such a delicate, sweet flower.

I bent to inhale her fragrance, loving the way her blood sang beneath my ministrations. She wanted me, just as she should. It was only natural to crave the touch of a superior.

Many took advantage of it.

Something I could so easily do now after she'd blatantly stated her desire to *please* me.

Maybe I should let her. Indulge the connection. Allow her to worship me at my feet for what little time she had left on this earth.

I ran my fingers through her hair once more, considering the option.

It was a dangerously attractive option. We weren't supposed to take humans away from their studies, but many of my kind offered private courses to increase a mortal's potential and worth.

That wasn't the same as claiming her or keeping her as mine.

Individual studies increased a human's value, making

them more attractive to the vampires and lycans who took mortals into their possession.

Maybe I could offer her my own form of training.

Then fail her entirely.

Write a personal recommendation to have her removed immediately for a lack of obedience.

I could even offer to be the one to terminate her.

I drew my knuckles down her cheek, considering the option and wondering why I hadn't thought of it before. Perhaps because she hadn't ever approached me about her scores.

That arguably showed courage.

A courage I would have to break.

Or maybe I would stoke it with fire, allow her to shine for a few brief moments in time, then reward her with death.

Students died every day.

No one cared.

I'd considered removing her before, but something about her wilting enthralled me.

Perhaps I should let her blossom just to destroy her.

A tempting idea. I cocked my head. "How badly do you want to pass my course, little flower? What position in society is it that you desire?"

She swallowed, her pupils dilating to cover those fiery embers in her irises. They'd only grown stronger in the last few minutes while I held her on her knees, staring down at her in mild contemplation.

"I want to go to the Immortal Cup," she told me, making me roll my eyes.

"All humans want that. Only twelve go a year. You think you're special enough to qualify?"

"I was. Before your class."

I snorted. She wasn't qualified for the Immortal Cup at all. And it had nothing to do with her scores.

The participants in the games were almost always preselected through genetic profiles. Unfortunately, my little flower didn't have what the superiors wanted for immortality. If she did, I would help her. But she'd been marked as harem material as her highest level of worth, mostly because of her body and pouty lips.

Not to mention her oral scores.

They were quite delicious, to the point that I'd almost given in to the desire to watch one of her exams.

But I'd had this irrational urge to murder the human she'd been assigned to perform on, and I'd forced myself to walk away.

Her eyes narrowed at me, momentarily distracting me from my thoughts. "My scores were perfect until your class."

"True," I agreed. "But they're not perfect now."

That fire touched her cheeks again, stirring a brilliant blush that crept all the way down her neck to the white T-shirt covering her breasts. I almost demanded that she remove the fabric, just so I could see how far the warmth went.

But she released a little noise that had my gaze jumping back up to her face.

A growl.

Her eyes widened, shock bleaching her features and chasing away the blush.

The little flower had just *growled* at me.

Fascinating.

I wanted to hear her do that with my cock lodged deep inside her. Make her growl and scream at the same time while her body fought the impulse to explode in rapture or jolt in fury.

I could picture it vividly.

And that image alone sealed her fate.

"You want to please me, little flower?" I asked, the question rhetorical now since I already knew the answer. "You want to try to pass my class?"

She started to nod, but I caught her throat, my palm squeezing as I forced her to remain still on her knees.

"I'll offer you an opportunity with private lessons," I told her. "But the moment you disobey me, I'll fail you on the spot. And I don't think I need to elaborate on what that means for you."

She didn't move or react other than to attempt to swallow against my hand.

"Take a day to think about it," I continued, my grip tightening just a little more to demonstrate the threat of her decision. "I'll expect your response after class tomorrow. And you can give it by staying behind, removing your clothes, and waiting for me on your knees on that mat." I pointed to the one she'd taken her test on just yesterday. "But if you accept my offer, you'd better be prepared to work for my approval. Because I won't go easy on you, darling."

My palm flexed a little more, cutting off her airflow as I held her gaze for several beats.

Her eyes widened.

Her cheeks went whiter than before.

And her lips parted in a clear desire to breathe.

I waited.

Counted a few more seconds, ensuring she understood the potential consequences of my offer.

Then I released her with a shove. "You're dismissed, Prospect."

I turned my back on her, not necessarily to be cruel, but because I didn't trust myself not to pounce on her.

That little growl of hers had nearly undone centuries of control.

She'd *tempted* me.

Even more than she already had.

An amazing feat, considering how badly I already wanted her.

But I'd give her this choice of fate.

She could spend the next nine months playing with me before her destined *Blood Day*.

Or she could take my class, fail, and see what designation she earned from the infamous Magistrate.

There was little I could do to help her in this world. I only wanted her death to be quick.

Because no one else deserved to see my flower wilt.

Only me.

She was my Lily.

Mine.

"Sleep well, little flower," I said as I heard her shuffling behind me. "And try not to dream. Fantasies don't exist in your world anymore."

LILY

MASTER CEDRIC'S WORDS WHIRLED THROUGH MY MIND ON repeat all the way to my room and deep into the morning hours.

"I'll offer you an opportunity with private lessons. But the moment you disobey me, I'll fail you on the spot. And I don't think I need to elaborate on what that means for you."

He didn't.

I knew exactly what that meant.

Death.

But he'd essentially promised me that by failing me in his course, too.

The question became, how far was I willing to go for a chance to survive?

My answer was easy—as far as it took.

He wanted me to kneel for him naked on a mat? So be it. I'd done far worse in my sexual arts courses.

So why can't I sleep? I wondered, squirming in my sheets. We were in the middle of the hot season, which meant the sun was almost unbearable during the day. And the dust clouds made it nearly impossible to see.

Fortunately, vampires were nocturnal.

Which meant Blood University operated on a night schedule.

Lycans apparently could do day or evening, but they didn't seem to mind operating beneath the stars. Probably because they preferred to avoid the warmth of the sun.

I could feel it peeking through my blinds now, heating my body to a near boiling point. *Similar to Master Cedric's touch.*

His palm around my throat had been terrifying.

And arousing.

Every time I swallowed, I remembered his hand against my skin, the heat of his palm singed into my memory. Vampires might have been walking undead, but that didn't make them cold.

Something Master Cedric had more than proved with his fingers and thumb.

I brushed my jaw, his residual energy a kiss to my senses. It was only in my head, but that didn't make it any less real to my thoughts.

"Try not to dream. Fantasies don't exist in your world anymore."

Then why did I want to fantasize about him? To dream about the way his irises had burned as he'd studied my mouth? To recall the intensity coming off his skin as he'd touched me?

My thighs clenched, my insides rolling with molten fire.

He'd done something to me. Wrapped me up in some sort of spell. Enchanted me in a manner that made me feel insane.

Or maybe I'd just lost my mind.

I growled at him, I marveled, rolling over to my other side. *What was I thinking?*

He'd just made me so frustrated.

And I'd reacted.

I'd thought surely my life was over in that moment,

that he would snap my neck for daring to disrespect him in such a manner. His dark gaze had heated severely, making me almost crave his lethal bite.

And then he'd offered me a choice.

A way out.

Well, not really.

Just an alternative to my fate. A way to *please* him. An opportunity I wouldn't refuse.

Close your eyes, I told myself. *Rest. You're going to need it.*

Because he wouldn't go easy on me.

He never did.

<hr />

I'd dreamt of him.

Perhaps it had been my subconscious's way of defying Master Cedric. Or maybe his final words had triggered the dream.

I'd been naked and on my knees, awaiting his final judgment.

Which had come in the form of a bite that spiraled me into an orgasmic state.

A state I still felt between my thighs now as I watched him demonstrate a new series of techniques. He was giving us our homework assignment, just as he did at the end of every class, telling us to return to our rooms and practice so that we could demonstrate them for him tomorrow.

Normally, I would rush right back to my small private space to do just that.

But I had an opportunity to accept.

"Remember, I expect precision and accuracy tomorrow," Master Cedric said, his gaze landing on me before addressing the rest of the class. "You're all dismissed."

No one stood around to ask questions.

No one spoke a single word.

Instead, they grabbed their bags, shuffled from the gymnasium-style classroom, and went on their way.

This was the last class of our night, ending just two hours before dawn. Most would stop by the cafeteria for their dinner bags—something I'd missed last night and regretted when I'd seen my small rations for breakfast— and would take their meals back to their rooms.

I would go without.

For him.

For a chance at surviving his course.

Although, he'd made it rather clear that he enjoyed watching me fail.

This was all probably a game to him, a way to taunt his prey. But I didn't have a choice. It was this or death, and I wasn't ready to embrace that yet—even though he'd suggested just yesterday that I should.

Recalling all his statements sent a shiver down my spine.

I made my choice, I reminded myself as I straightened my shoulders. *This is what needs to be done. Strip. Kneel. Beg. Whatever he requires.*

Stripping wasn't a problem—I often had to remove my clothes for class or other activities.

Kneeling wasn't an issue either—I prayed on my knees to the Goddess before breakfast daily. It was a required activity for all the humans, to chant our thanks for allowing us to live.

Begging would be more difficult, primarily because I didn't know what Master Cedric wanted from me other than failure.

And failure wasn't in my repertoire.

I removed my clothes, as he'd told me to do, and fell

into a submissive kneeling pose on the mat—thighs slightly spread apart, hands behind my back, and head bowed. Sometimes the Masters required us to sit back on our heels, but I wasn't sure if he preferred that or not. So I knelt with my thighs and upper body perpendicular to the floor while keeping my eyes downcast as a show of respect.

Then I waited.

And waited.

And waited.

I started counting seconds, then minutes, and eventually just focused on my breathing.

Master Cedric hadn't left, his presence a dark shadow in the room. However, I sensed his focus wasn't on me. I couldn't say how or why I knew that, just that I felt free to breathe for the moment because those cruel, cold eyes weren't directed my way.

Was this a test? A way to ensure my resolve?

I could remain like this for hours; I'd done it before.

But surely he wouldn't force me to remain in this pose all day. The windows of this room overlooked one of the campus's many deserts, marking it a prime location for sunshine.

I would melt in here.

Become dehydrated and pass out.

Maybe that was his intention.

I swallowed, uncertain of how long I would last under those circumstances. Not with how little I'd eaten over the last twenty-four hours and how terribly I'd slept last night.

"Let's see how well you were paying attention today, Prospect," Master Cedric said, his tone and words causing goose bumps to pebble up and down my arms. "Show me tonight's lesson. We'll see how poor your technique is and go from there."

My heart raced in my chest. *Tonight's lesson. The*

assignment he gave us for practice. He'd just executed it twice for us to memorize.

I usually practiced these dozens of times before performing in front of him.

And he wanted me to do this without any practice at all.

"Now, little flower," he demanded.

Little flower. I wasn't sure why he kept calling me that. I'd never heard him say it to anyone in class. But I wasn't going to waste time evaluating it now. Not when he gave me an assignment to fulfill.

I carefully found my footing while recalling everything he'd shown us and fell into the appropriate fighting stance. The routine he'd demonstrated today wasn't long, just a series of kicks and punches in quick succession. It was all about the footing and hip movement, something I'd always studied carefully throughout each lesson.

So I focused on that now, moving my feet along the floor in a dance similar to his and putting the appropriate effort behind my throws and swift leg thrusts. One of the positions required a knee tuck that I executed with a bit of a wobble, but Master Cedric didn't say anything until I completed the final tumble.

"Again," he told me.

I didn't argue. I didn't even hesitate. I merely went back to the starting position and ran through the routine once more.

Then I repeated it a third time on his command.

And a fourth.

And a fifth.

But it wasn't until the sixth attempt that I actually felt his eyes on me, his stare resembling a brand that imprinted itself on my soul.

I stumbled in response, earning a snort from him.

Rather than pause, I kept going, my cheeks on fire from the exertion and knowing I'd fumbled beneath his penetrating gaze.

I quickly started on a seventh turn, running through the routine this time with flawless ease and feeling the perfection in each step.

But when I lifted my focus to him, hoping to see pride in his expression, I found him glaring at me instead. "You're already dead, Prospect."

My brow furrowed. I didn't understand what he meant.

He dropped something on his desk and started toward me, his intense expression sending a chill of foreboding over my spirit. *Don't,* I told myself as I nearly took a step backward, my instinct to flee thundering through my veins. *Don't run.*

It was what excited predators.

They enjoyed stalking and hunting prey.

If I remained still, he might not try to kill me.

Although, he'd already claimed me to be dead.

So maybe not.

He grabbed my hips and moved me back into the position where I'd lost my balance, then he swept my bent leg out from beneath me and sent me down hard to the mat.

His body landed on mine in the next breath, his lips at my neck, his hands holding my wrists over my head to capture me beneath him.

I jolted, my heart suddenly in my throat. *Goddess…*

But he hadn't come down hard on me. He'd moved rather stealthily, his weight balanced more on his knees as he straddled my legs. Then he'd melted into me on the floor with his thighs pressing on mine and his torso fully covering me.

All within the course of a few seconds.

However, it was enough to soften the tackle after knocking the wind from my lungs with his leg sweep.

Almost as though he was trying not to truly hurt me.

A weird thought, one that probably wasn't right at all. This vampire hated me. He wanted to fail me. Why would he treat me kindly on the floor?

His lips brushed my neck, his resulting hum trickling over my skin and setting my blood on fire for him. I almost tilted my head, my instinct to give in to his vampiric kiss one practically trained into me from birth.

He didn't bite me.

He merely pressed his lips to my throat and held me beneath him with ease.

My eyes fell shut, resignation falling over me as I submitted to him the way a human should.

Which earned me a tsk from his lips. "A single error in execution would end in your death every time, sweet flower," he whispered, his mouth traveling up to my ear. "You're too delicate, too *weak*, for combat. Whether against me, or against your own. It's not the right path for you."

He gathered my wrists beneath one hand, holding my arms over my head as he lowered his opposite hand to my throat.

I shivered as he moved back to stare down at me with those cold, dark orbs. "You wouldn't survive a single day in the Immortal Cup, Prospect. Even with perfect execution, you would die. That's why you'll always fail." His focus fell to my mouth as I bit my lower lip to keep from reacting.

Except that was a reaction in itself.

A telling one, too.

Because his words pierced a part of me that didn't want to hear his assessment. His cruelty. His promise for failure.

I was smaller than the others—a petite female of only

five feet, four inches. And the compound kept me thin by regulating my daily intake of calories.

But I wanted to be strong.

To fight.

To be a human of worth, not a sexual servant or a blood slave.

How could I change my fate when vampires like Master Cedric refused to teach me? How could I improve my strength without more energy?

I'd witnessed so many others in my position give up and succumb to their fates.

I refused.

I wanted to prove my worth, to be the human I knew I could be with proper training.

It was why I'd enrolled myself in his course.

"I can do this," I told him. "I can perfect my skills and perform flawless executions of your techniques." I wasn't sure where my boldness had come from, or what had provoked my words of confidence, but I didn't apologize for speaking so bluntly.

Because there was nothing else for me to lose.

He'd threatened to fail me, had proved his point by easily taking me down to the floor.

But that didn't mean I couldn't try again, that I couldn't *learn* to be better.

His gaze narrowed, a dark emotion I couldn't define lurking in his inky irises. He didn't move or speak, just continued to study me as though testing my resolve. Perhaps like he'd done when I'd gone to my knees.

I wasn't a quitter.

I was a fighter.

And I would continue fighting until my dying breath.

"We'll see," he finally said after a beat. "Same time tomorrow. Same position. Don't disappoint me, Prospect."

He released me in a fluid motion, rolling off of me and up to his feet in a blink.

Vampire, I thought, swallowing at the graceful movement. He'd moved faster than my mind could comprehend, his strength and agility far superior to my own.

And yet he'd been almost gentle with me on the floor.

How strange.

"Good night, little flower," he murmured as he returned to his desk. "Don't forget your clothes."

My lips parted at the not-so-subtle reminder of my nude state.

I'd completely forgotten about stripping for him before practicing my positions. Performing the fighting sequence had taken over my thoughts, making me forget about my lack of clothing.

But I was very aware of it now.

More aware than I'd ever been.

Because he'd been on top of me, holding me to the ground while I was naked. Which meant he'd felt my nipples pebbling beneath him. He'd probably scented my submissive arousal as well.

It was only natural to react to his presence.

Although, my reaction to him had certainly been more potent than usual. Probably because he was among the first of his kind to actually touch me. I never volunteered in sexual studies for demonstrations with the superiors; I preferred to watch and perform on other humans.

Just as I usually sparred with mortals in Master Cedric's class.

Until tonight.

Until he watched me perform seven times while naked before flattening me to the floor.

"Prospect?" Master Cedric prompted, his eyebrow arching. "Did that little tumble disrupt your hearing?"

"N-no, Master," I said, jumping up from the ground to begin dressing.

Only, I moved too fast and the world began to spin, causing me to lose my footing.

His arm caught my waist in the next instant, holding me upright when I would have fallen, his vampiric speed taking my breath away.

I shuddered as his minty scent washed over me, his hard body eliciting forbidden yearnings deep within.

For a moment, I wondered how I would react to him needing a volunteer in a sexual arts class. He might just tempt me to raise my hand.

A foolish notion.

Because he would probably choke me to a point of unconsciousness. Then fail me for not being able to swallow.

But the potential to see him in that way, to taste him, suddenly appealed to me a lot more than it should.

His arm tightened around me, his palm going to the nape of my neck as he pulled my head back to gaze up at him. A slight frown creased his brow, his dark eyes a little less cold. Or maybe that was an illusion. A dream.

A fantasy for later.

Maybe.

I felt pretty light-headed.

Like I might just fall asleep right now.

"Lily." Master Cedric's voice held a strange note to it. Not chilling or cruel like usual. But an odd deepness that made me warm all over. Except I didn't understand his comment. He seemed to always be talking about flowers.

And fighting.

And death.

And failing me.

I tried to shake my head, but that only made my dizziness worse.

"When was the last time you ate something?" he asked.

"Breakfast bag," I replied, my voice a bit hoarse.

He sighed. "And you've already missed dinner."

"Did I miss it again?" I wondered out loud, uncertain of the time. *Probably,* I thought. The window for picking up food was very strict, and he'd likely kept me too long for tonight's session.

His scent slithered around me as he pressed another kiss to my pulse. "So delicate and fragile," he whispered. "My sweet Lily flower."

My lips nearly curled down, but I caught the instinct at the last moment before I could react.

Reactions weren't allowed.

Humans who screamed—*died*.

Humans who showed displeasure—*died*.

Humans who displayed anything other than contentment or boredom—*died*.

My stomach rumbled then, stirring another wave of dizziness. He'd told me to get dressed and leave, but I couldn't move with his arm trapping me against him.

I swallowed, uncertain of how to proceed.

Then he slowly led me to the chair behind his desk. It was the only furniture in the room aside from the mats. "Sit," he said, his tone oddly soft.

I started to move toward the ground but found my hips in his hands as he directed me to the chair.

My eyes widened, as this position was one I shouldn't be taking. My legs nearly gave out, my body automatically trying to retreat to the floor, but his grip around my hips tightened in response.

"Don't. Move." His command thundered over me,

locking me in place against the leather. "Do you remember what I said about disobeying me, Prospect?"

My stomach twisted. *I disobeyed him by not getting dressed and leaving.* Which meant… "You'll fail me." Because that was his threat.

"The moment you disobey me, I'll fail you on the spot."

Those were his exact words.

My lips parted, my gaze falling to his desk.

"Yes, Prospect. That's exactly what I said." He released my hips and placed his hands on the arms of the chair to lean down, caging me between him and the leather at my back. "So stay here like an obedient little pet and don't fucking move."

With that pronouncement, he pushed away from me, turned off the lights, and disappeared from the room.

Which left me shaking in his chair.

Alone in his classroom.

Abandoned after curfew.

Without my clothes.

In the dark.

CEDRIC

"I NEED A DINNER BAG," I SAID AS I MATERIALIZED IN THE campus kitchens.

The human servant beside me did her best to hide a yelp at my sudden appearance, but I'd heard it with my enhanced hearing. Some of my kind would enjoy punishing her for the reaction. It served as a way to keep ourselves superior and the mortals meek.

However, society had already done the job of degrading humankind to cattle, so I didn't see the benefit of belaboring the point.

This whole bloody operation felt trivial to me.

What was wrong with hunting and seducing our food? Why did we have to make it so easy and boring?

Alas, it wasn't for me to make those decisions.

I merely served the system.

Well, not exactly. My expertise was requested to fill a recent opening, and I'd agreed as a way to escape the political pressures of Silvano Region. My maker—Prince Silvano himself—wanted to promote me to a sovereign position. And I just wasn't interested.

So I'd opted for the Blood University role instead.

Which had afforded me the opportunity to meet my Lily—a temptation I'd never known I craved.

"What kind of dinner bag, Sire?" the human servant asked.

She wasn't a student but a mortal chosen for this task after what was likely a grueling Blood Day experience. That event was the proverbial graduation ceremony for Blood University students—a day when all mortals were assigned their fates.

To end up here meant this human had been sent to the servant auction first, then purchased specifically to spend the rest of her mortal days in a kitchen.

Then she'd been processed for *this* kitchen.

I eyed her curiously, noting the graying hairs along her scalp and the subtle wrinkles beneath her eyes.

It was on the tip of my tongue to ask her age because she'd obviously matured past her prime years—a feat accomplished by essentially living in a safe area not commonly frequented by superior beings. Lycans needed food, while vampires did not. And lycans were less prone to the sudden desire to drain a mortal of their life essence.

Interesting, I mused, still scrutinizing her as an idea formed in my mind.

However, the mortal began to shake—another outward reaction that could earn her an immediate death sentence —drawing me from my musings.

"There are different types of dinner bags?" I asked, not at all familiar with how these kitchens operated. I knew they existed to provide necessary sustenance for the human students. But there had never been a cause for me to visit —hence this human's break in her programming. She likely hadn't seen a vampire in several years, her position here keeping her secluded and safe.

Which only had me returning to the idea blossoming in my mind.

Maybe my sweet Lily flower could end up here instead of in a grave.

"Y-yes," the mortal stammered, her nervous behavior enthralling me.

How are you still alive? I marveled. *When was the last time you saw a vampire?* There weren't many on campus. Maybe two dozen of us and three dozen lycans. All of the supernatural beings were here to teach the mortals how to perform as suitable cattle.

There were also another two or three dozen lycans in charge of managing the humans in personal areas, such as in the dormitories.

And then the human Vigils guarded the school grounds, hunting and killing their own kind when one was stupid enough to try to escape.

However, that wasn't common.

The real reason Vigils existed on these grounds was to provide the mortals with a false sense of hope. The Vigils resembled a position the humans could aspire to attain, thus giving them a reason to cooperate and compete against each other.

Manipulative programming.

A dark new age of mortal existence.

And boring as fuck for vampires like me who missed the hunt.

The mortal began listing the dinner bag options by body type, not by contents.

It was a good regimen designed by gender and desired weight. I suspected sweet Lily was in the lower-weight section, given her petite frame. But she possessed natural curves that might have increased her food intake level by just a bit. And if not, then her classification should be reevaluated because her curves were absolutely perfect.

Actually, everything about her was perfect.

Her determination.

Her subtle defiance.

Her alluring fear.

She was probably sitting in my classroom with her heart racing and her skin prickled with goose bumps.

So pretty and small.

And mine.

Clearing my throat, I pushed away that last possessive thought and selected a dinner bag at the top weight class. She needed some extra food after missing her meal last night. And it seemed she didn't qualify for lunch bags, which was another weight management technique used to force the cattle to achieve a desired appearance.

"Thank you," I said to the human.

Her eyes rounded in response.

Just because vampires were superior didn't mean we couldn't be polite.

Of course, *Goddess* Lilith wouldn't approve. She'd berate me and remind me of my duty to be dismissive of those beneath us.

"It's a service, really. We don't want them to gain hope. That's just cruel," she'd say.

I nearly rolled my eyes as I phased back to my building.

All the humans bowed and prayed to Lilith as though she were some supreme being. It was another ploy to force submission among the weaker-minded.

Give the humans a deity to pray to.

Only, Lilith wasn't a Goddess at all. Just a supreme bitch with a power complex.

Nyx was the true Goddess of our kind, the one worthy of daily worship.

I often wondered how she felt about Lilith taking on her role and pretending to be the divine incarnate.

But that wasn't my problem to ponder. If Nyx disliked the representation, she'd find a way to let Lilith know.

I rather wished Nyx would do so soon, as I was quite tired of waking up to the humans reciting the Lilith prayer every evening.

All thoughts of Nyx and Lilith disappeared when I entered my classroom to find Lily in the chair I'd left her in. She hadn't moved an inch, her submissive gaze on my desk as she held her body absolutely still.

Such a good little flower, I thought, moving toward her on silent feet.

The lights were off, leaving her protected by darkness.

No one would think to enter this room without my permission, keeping her temporarily safe from others of my kind. If only I could find a permanent solution.

I wanted to be the one to watch her wilt. No one else.

But that was a problem to solve another day.

Right now, I just needed her to eat.

I set the bag down on my desk and noted the shiver cascading across her bare skin. She didn't appear to be fazed at all by her nudity, something she'd likely grown accustomed to over the years.

But I was very much affected by her bare state.

All that creamy skin, subtly toned muscle, and her delicate curves made my mouth water.

It'd taken serious restraint not to bite her when I'd pinned her to the floor. I'd wanted to taste her essence, then kiss and nibble my way down her exquisite body to the alluring haven between her thighs.

Alas, it would be too easy to take her.

She'd submit to me because she was trained to submit.

And I found that I craved something more from my Lily—*desire*.

I wanted her to beg me to fuck her because she wanted me, not because she felt obligated to accept me.

A dream, I supposed.

Humans weren't able to express their hopes and desires anymore.

Which left me yearning for a fantasy I would never truly experience.

"You did very well, little flower," I informed her softly as I went through the bag of food.

It included a balanced meal of seasonless grilled meat and vegetables and a small tin of plain rice. There was a banana for dessert.

And two bottles of water.

Not the most appetizing food in the world.

But Lily wouldn't know that. She and all the humans here were trained to eat and accept bland food.

I took each item out and placed them on my desk, then picked up the fork and speared a cut-up piece of chicken. "Open," I said, bringing the food to her mouth.

Her eyes darted up to mine in the dark, allowing me to see the surprise in her expression. Maybe she thought the lights being off hid her reactions. Or perhaps she was too stunned to mask her shock.

Either way, I was thankful for the experience. Because those pretty blue-green irises sparkled with emotion, making me wonder what else I could evoke from her.

Pleasure?

Pain?

Excitement?

All of those options held an unmistakable allure.

But I settled on her surprise for now.

And enjoyed watching her comply with my command.

The fork disappeared between her parted lips, her mouth instantly taking the offered food from the prongs.

I picked out a green bean from her vegetable mix to feed her next, purposely slowing my movements with the fork to allow her enough time to chew and swallow.

She parted her lips automatically when I brought the food to her mouth, allowing me to feed her without the requisite command.

We didn't speak throughout the process, her body reacting to my care on instinct alone.

I opened the water to give her a drink, then continued with more meat and vegetables before serving her some rice.

Her gaze remained on me, perhaps trying to see me in the dark. Moonlight bathed the windows in eerie shadows, likely allowing her to at least observe the outlines of my features. Or maybe she could see me clearly now that her eyes had become accustomed to the dark.

It'd been so long since I was human that I couldn't remember the extent of my former senses. However, her pupils were dilated so widely now that her irises were thin circles of color around the big black orbs.

If she could see me, she was being rather bold by studying my features.

But I wasn't going to discipline her for it.

Instead, I sat back against my desk and continued feeding her. Every time I brought the bottle to her lips, her nostrils flared. Did she worry that I might drown her with it? I supposed some of my kind would.

Her cheeks flushed when I offered her the banana.

It was an erotic sight to watch the tip disappear between her lips. I allowed it to remain there for a prolonged moment while I fantasized about having my cock in that sweet mouth instead.

Then I gave her more water to wash down the sweet fruit.

She swallowed, her cheeks still pink.

And the sweetest scent of arousal touched the air.

Her arousal.

I inhaled deeply, welcoming the floral fragrance into my lungs and humming my approval on my exhale.

She squirmed in response, her first true movement other than eating since my return.

My lips curled as I gave her the banana again.

Her eyes seemed to hold mine as she accepted it, her cheeks burning even more. I could feel the heat rolling off her, and it had nothing to do with the miserably hot weather outside.

She bit off another piece, chewed, and then swallowed.

Beautiful.

I swapped the banana for her water and brought the bottle to my lips rather than hers. My dry throat needed relief, but the liquid did little to soothe it.

So I held some of the water in my mouth instead and bent to press my lips to hers.

She quivered in response, her floral scent increasing in intensity. Then she opened for me and allowed me to share the water with her in an intimate kiss of refreshing warmth.

I lingered long enough for her to swallow, then pulled back to give her the rest of the drink via the bottle.

Mostly because I didn't trust myself not to do more.

It wouldn't necessarily be a problem if I did. Students disappeared often as a result of lust and temptation.

I was honestly surprised no one had tried to take her yet.

So sweet and fragile. A beautiful flower in bloom with long stems and delicate skin.

Mmm.

I fed her the last part of the banana before opening her other water. She drank half of it, clearly dehydrated. But she paused near the end, her gaze holding a secret I didn't quite understand.

"You're still thirsty," I said, finally breaking our silence. "Why did you stop drinking?"

"If I'm going back to my room, then I would prefer to take it with me. I often wake up thirsty from the heat."

I frowned at that. Of course she would wake up thirsty. This place was a literal hellhole in the northeastern part of the Sahara Desert.

No one wanted to live here, which was why only a few vampires and lycans agreed to teach at the universities. There were ten around the world, all of them located in inhospitable regions.

I just happened to prefer this over political games.

For now, anyway.

"Finish this bottle," I told her, ensuring she knew it was a demand and not a request.

She obeyed, her throat eager, but I caught a note of fear in her scent. It was an intoxicating perfume that called to my inner predator. But I swallowed my urge and busied myself with cleaning up after her finished meal. Everything was biodegradable, including her fork, which made it easy to discard the products in my classroom's trash bin.

Lily didn't move while I worked, her obedience resolute as she waited for my next command.

I nearly told her to lie on my desk with her legs spread so I could indulge myself in some dessert.

"Get dressed" was what came out instead.

Rather than watch her obey, I walked to the closet at the back of my classroom and unlocked it with my thumbprint. A few essentials lurked inside, including a case of chilled water in a fridge. I grabbed four bottles—two for each hand—and brought them back to Lily just as she finished pulling on her plain white shirt.

All the prospects wore the same clothes—plain colors, either pants or shorts or skirts, and T-shirts.

When she attended her sexual arts classes, she typically wore nothing at all.

My class mandated shirts and pants for physical exercises.

Which she knew.

Yet she hadn't thought to put her clothes back on while practicing her exercises tonight.

And I hadn't bothered to correct her. Now I'd require her nudity going forward. Because it pleased me and that suited her goals.

Her eyes widened again upon noticing the items in my hands, confirming she could see in the dark. So she had to know I could see her, too.

But she didn't try to mask her reactions.

I liked that.

It pleased me almost as much as her naked performance earlier.

"Take these with you," I told her, giving her the bottles. "I expect you to drink at least two of them before breakfast."

She'd almost fainted on me as a result of starvation and dehydration. I didn't want that to happen again.

"Yes, Master Cedric."

That right there was perhaps the only enjoyable element of this whole new world order—the way Lily called me *Master*. It made me hard every fucking time.

If only she meant it in the way a woman should—while playing in the bedroom. Alas, that time had passed.

"Go back to your room, Prospect." The words came

out a little harsher than I'd intended, mostly due to my own personal frustration. "We will continue your lessons after class tomorrow." I pointed to the mat. "Same place. Same position. No clothes."

She swallowed. "Yes, Master Cedric," she whispered, bowing her head slightly.

But she didn't immediately move.

Instead, she nibbled her lip, her gaze going to the water I'd given her.

I arched a brow. "I'm starting to question your hearing again, Prospect."

She outwardly shivered, her eyes darting up to mine before falling again. "Sorry, Master Cedric. I…" She trailed off, causing both my eyebrows to lift in astonishment. Most humans would have run off by now, eager to obey. But not Lily.

"Do you wish to say something?" I asked, testing her.

She nodded. "Yes."

Most would consider that response to be a failure— humans weren't allowed to speak unless directly told to do so. But she was essentially saying she wanted to voice a thought.

And for me, that meant she'd passed.

"Speak freely," I said, rewarding her boldness.

It was a dangerous response on my part, one that could earn her a death sentence later should she choose to behave this way in front of the wrong vampire or lycan.

Hence the reason I wanted her life to end early, to ensure her beautiful soul wasn't tarnished too severely by what this world had become.

However, I would enjoy this side of her now and forever cherish the memory of my sweet flower.

At least until time erased her from my thoughts.

"I wanted to say 'thank you.'" Her words were soft. "For the meal and the water."

My jaw ticked. She was thanking me for keeping her alive—the opposite of what I truly desired. And yet the words tasted so sweet on her lips.

I was torn between growling and smiling.

So I said nothing at all.

Because I didn't trust myself not to strangle her.

Or fuck her against a wall.

Maybe both.

Such a dangerous conflict of interest.

"Good night, Master Cedric," she whispered, smartly backing away from me and heading toward the door with her gaze on the floor.

She likely sensed my conflict. Perhaps even felt my need to kill her.

That would explain the heightening of her pulse.

However, she left a hint of that arousing fragrance behind, the intoxicating perfume circling me and begging me to chase her.

To hunt her.

To claim her.

She was my chosen prey.

One day I might just give in to this urge to take her. Devour her. Bleed her dry.

But not today.

"Sleep well, Lily," I whispered after her, aware that she couldn't actually hear me. "You're going to need it."

Because tomorrow I would show her just why she could never become a Vigil.

A lesson in delicacy and strength.

A lesson that she would absolutely fail.

My poor sweet flower.

May you bloom again another day.

LILY

I couldn't stop thinking about Master Cedric's banana and the way he'd fed it to me last night.

Maybe because I was on my knees in sexual arts class with a similar object in my mouth.

An object I kept envisioning as belonging to Master Cedric and not the human male standing before me.

I focused on swirling my tongue, but each swipe resembled a lick between my bare thighs.

Because I kept picturing Master Cedric.

It was his fingers in my hair. His salty essence in my mouth. His groan vibrating the air.

I could picture it so perfectly.

All because of that banana.

And the kiss that had followed.

Maybe it hadn't really been a kiss. But his lips had touched mine when he'd given me that water. It was a moment that had stolen my breath away. An entire experience that I'd never known was possible.

He'd *fed* me.

Given me several nights of food.

Then multiple bottles of water.

Oh, it'd been cool water, too. I'd never tasted such heavenly liquid before.

Another groan reverberated through my partner, his grip tightening in my hair.

"Don't come," Master Peyton said in a silky voice, her nails gliding along the neck of Prospect Four Hundred and Six. I called him Six for short, just as he called me Sev.

Six and I were often paired in our courses because of our number sequence being one off from the other. We were both the same year. Which meant we would attend our Blood Day together.

His light green eyes pleaded with me to slow my pace, to ensure he met Master Peyton's orders.

But my task was to make him fall apart with my mouth.

It provided a cruel conflict that meant one of us had to lose.

And I wasn't going to fail.

Not when I kept envisioning Master Cedric's midnight irises glistening with dark intent as he'd slid that banana between my lips.

I could so easily pretend this was him, that he'd demanded I kneel and *please* him.

It would be a sexual performance he wished for me to repeat, not a fight sequence.

And just the thought of that coated my thighs in damp intrigue.

This had never happened to me before. I never felt aroused by the act of giving fellatio. But thinking about Master Cedric made my core throb with forbidden need.

He would never be mine.

I shouldn't romanticize him or lust after him.

All vampires were inherently seductive. It was part of their predatory appeal. Even Master Peyton possessed a flawless appearance with her pretty black hair and olive-toned skin. She smiled at me now, clearly enjoying this show of sensual torment.

Six didn't stand a chance.

He was so worked up, his shaft pulsating in my mouth in clear warning.

Master Peyton chastised him, but it didn't matter.

He exploded on a growl that caused all the hairs along my neck to stand on end.

Would Master Cedric growl, too? Would he fist my hair and thrust himself deeper? How would he taste? Salty like Six? Would I drown in his pleasure? Or would it be over quickly, similar to this experience now?

So many dangerous questions.

I swallowed them all with Six's essence, my mind picturing Master Cedric instead of the male before me.

I felt dizzy and hot, my body aching for someone I shouldn't crave.

But that kiss last night.

The way he'd fed me.

The care of his touch.

The heat in his gaze.

It'd all provoked a yearning inside me I couldn't quite ignore, and I'd taken it out on Six. Which left me feeling empty and oddly unsteady.

Incomplete.

Wrong.

"Well done, Prospect Four Hundred and Seven," Master Peyton praised, her sharp nails threading through Six's thick auburn hair. "Come with me, Prospect Four Hundred and Six."

He swallowed, his pink cheeks going white.

She was about to make an example of him by making him come again in front of the class.

By using her fangs.

I'd seen it done a few times now. Master Peyton called it a training process to help the loser of these games learn orgasm control.

It wasn't something I'd been subjected to yet, as I hadn't failed any of my tests. However, that likely had more to do with the course's design than my actual skill.

The males always lost these games, something I suspected was a result of Master Peyton preferring men.

All of her demonstrations were on the males, never the females. And she always touched the men during our tests, not the women.

The wheels of Master Peyton's chair whirled across the floor as she shoved Six into the seat. It was much harsher than what Master Cedric had done to me last night. Just as Master Peyton's movements now were far more predatory than Master Cedric's had been.

"Don't make a sound," Master Peyton demanded as she went to her knees.

Then she lowered her head to Six's groin.

I held my breath, praying to the Goddess that Six obeyed her command. Because I'd seen what had happened last week when the previous male hadn't remained quiet.

He wasn't present today.

He'd failed.

And I suspected he was now dead.

Since this course happened only once every seven days, I hadn't been sure of his fate. But given his absence, it seemed likely that Master Peyton had finished the job of killing him.

Fortunately, Six didn't make a sound.

But his face expressed an agony that made my heart squeeze in my chest.

Master Peyton would continue until she felt his training was sufficient.

Or until the bell dismissed us.

We all had one more class before our free day began.

It happened once a week after our fullest class day.

I had four primary courses at the moment. One was a political course about the royal vampires of the world— this one happened twice a week.

Then I had a hospitality course and Master Cedric's course, both of which occurred six days a week.

The hospitality course was considered to be a vocational focus class, while Master Cedric's combat training counted as my required daily physical activity.

Sexual arts and my political lessons were considered general education courses, both of which were required but taken at a time of my choosing.

Or that was how my advisor had phrased it.

She was a vampire I'd never actually met in person, but we spoke via a telecommunication screen on a monthly basis. She always reviewed my current marks and curriculum, then shifted my classes around as needed to meet certain requirements.

I never fully understood those requirements, though. She just gave me options and let me pick what I wanted to study.

And lately, she'd been pushing sexual arts as my general education choices.

I was required to take a certain amount before my Blood Day, and I hadn't met that expectation yet.

So here I was, still on my knees, watching Six silently scream.

By the time the bell rang, I felt numb.

Six was moving, but he appeared just as pale as the

male from last week. His cheeks were sunken. His irises were more yellow than green. And his legs were unsteady.

I rinsed out my mouth with the requisite supplies at the back of the locker room before moving to my designated locker to pull on my clothes.

Six stood beside me, his movements slow and his gaze downcast. He seemed to be struggling to pull up his black jeans. Then his fingers trembled so hard that he couldn't do up his zipper or button his pants, so I reached over to do it for him.

He grumbled something that sounded more like a "Fuck you" than a "Thank you." But I didn't take offense to it. I understood his anger. I accepted it. And I helped him pull his shirt over his head even while he glared at me.

We both knew the rules here.

We existed to survive.

I'd done exactly that. He would forgive me eventually. Or he wouldn't. That decision wouldn't really matter in a few months after our Blood Day anyway.

Six tried to bend to put on his shoes and flinched violently.

So I went to the ground and helped him.

He didn't grumble this time, but I could see the misery in his features as I stood again. There was a hint of understanding there as well, along with a note of embarrassment, and maybe a little envy.

I slipped his bag up over his shoulder, then retrieved my own from my locker.

His gaze locked on mine for a long moment, a myriad of emotions escaping his yellow-green irises.

I waited, knowing he needed this—an outlet he could confide in without words.

After a few dark seconds, he swallowed and cleared the reaction from his features. I held out my arm, which he accepted, and I helped him out the door, neither of us uttering a word to each other along the way.

Then we parted ways for our final course of the day.

He wasn't in Master Cedric's combat training. I didn't actually know what Six's next class was because it had nothing to do with me.

However, a small part of me hoped he made it safely through to his rest day tomorrow.

We weren't friends, as fraternization was frowned upon here. But we were allies of a sort, and I'd known him all my life.

To lose an acquaintance after twenty-one years would be disappointing. Especially when we were so close to the end of our time here.

Hopefully, he would recover.

Taking a deep breath, I pushed Six from my mind. I needed to focus on my next task—Master Cedric's combat training.

I'm not failing another test, I decided, ready to face him once more.

I'd practiced several times after returning to my room following our late-night session. And I'd practiced this morning as well.

I'm ready.

This time, he wouldn't be able to fail me.

I'd prove my worth and make him see my potential.

Then I'd strip for him once more and wait on the mat for our private lesson.

And try very hard not to think about his banana.

LILY

Master Cedric was already in the room when I arrived, his long legs casually crossed at the ankles as he leaned back against his desk.

It was the same position he'd taken last night while he'd fed me, only he was facing the classroom today instead of his chair.

His strong hands were gripping the wood beneath him, his gaze cold as he surveyed the students entering the room.

When his eyes found mine, I shivered, the intensity radiating off of him making my knees go weak. I immediately lowered my focus to the floor, taking on a demure pose of required respect.

I shouldn't have even made eye contact with him to begin with.

Alas, I seemed to be forgetting a lot of the rules where he was concerned.

Swallowing, I set my bag off to the side, kicked off my shoes and socks, and found my usual mat. Except a snap of Master Cedric's fingers pulled my attention to him once more. "Prospect Four Hundred and Seven, I want you to work with Prospect Six Hundred and Forty-Two today."

What? I glanced at the human in question, noting his hulking size.

"*Now*, Prospect," Master Cedric added when I didn't immediately move.

I jumped to obey, but my heart stuttered in my throat. Because this guy had at least a foot on my five-foot-four frame, and his arms were the size of my thighs.

To be fair, most of the men in this class were like that.

There were ones larger than Prospect Six Hundred and Forty-Two, too.

But I usually sparred with the only other girl in the class—whom Master Cedric was now pairing up with this prospect's usual fighting partner.

I shared a glance with the female, her expression showcasing how I felt about this development. It was a quick look, but we were both taken aback by this new pairing.

Of course, she always passed our assignments, while I always failed.

So she likely blamed me for this.

Which was probably accurate.

Only, I thought maybe things would be a bit different after last night. Master Cedric had been almost kind to me.

I'd thought I was in trouble after not immediately complying with his demand; he'd left me naked on that chair for what had felt like a half hour. I'd wondered if he would actually come back.

Then he'd returned with food.

And fed me.

Why had he done that?

"We are going to start with technique execution," he announced as the final two students entered the room.

"You'll perform the routine from the last class. Then you're going to use at least four moves from that sequence against your sparring partner."

Well, that didn't sound too bad.

"While your partner actively defends against your attack," he added, his words sending a chill through my being. "There will be no rules or limits today. Defend yourselves as you see fit, and you are welcome to execute more than four moves on the offensive as well. Four is the minimum."

He clapped, and the sound resembled thunder to my ears.

No rules or limits.

Sparring moves with open defense.

Against a male twice my size.

I looked at my new partner and noted the stoicism in his features. He wasn't fazed by this at all. Actually, he appeared a bit bored.

Which, yeah. He'd just been assigned a mouse to beat up. If I were him, I'd be bored, too.

"Prospect Four Hundred and Seven, I want you to go first," Master Cedric announced before addressing the rest of the class. "You all have five minutes to warm up, starting now."

So he wasn't giving me time to mentally prepare for this change either. Or maybe he didn't want me to psych myself out.

Either way, I took his command and ran with it—literally—by doing three laps around the room before falling into my usual stretching routine.

My mind calmed with each movement, my body leading the way without much thought.

All the other students followed suit, everyone preparing themselves for today's class.

After stretching, I went through two practice rounds of the fighting sequence before taking my position on the mat, ready to perform.

Master Cedric remained by his desk, still leaning with his ankles crossed, his hands tucked into his pockets. "Time's up," he said, his cold gaze landing on me. "Begin."

I didn't hesitate, falling into the first move and executing the routine just like yesterday. Only this time, I wore a pair of black stretchy pants and a white T-shirt.

And I executed each move flawlessly.

Not that Master Cedric agreed or even commented. Instead, he gestured at Prospect Six Hundred and Forty-Two to demonstrate the same movements.

I studied his kicks and punches, wincing when I realized how much power he packed behind each movement.

He's going to break me in half, I realized as he finished the performance with a deadly chop through the air.

Master Cedric nodded, dismissing us to the side. Then he called upon my usual partner and her new sparring mate. They went through the movements, the male just as intimidating as the one standing beside me.

I swallowed, my heart racing harder and harder as each pair went through their routines until the class came full circle and returned to me.

"Prospect Four Hundred and Seven will be on the offensive first," Master Cedric declared. "Only defensive moves, Prospect Six Hundred and Forty-Two."

The beastly male dipped his chin in acknowledgment.

This is going to end badly.

It was sort of reminiscent of my last class, where one opponent had to fail. Only, Master Cedric wouldn't torture the loser the way Master Peyton had.

He'd just let the loser break and leave him or her to heal alone.

"Begin." Impatience darkened Master Cedric's tone.

He must have sensed my hesitation because he bit off the word the moment my feet touched the mat. I wasn't even in a fighting stance yet, but my sparring partner appeared prepared as he put his fists up to block me.

I started with a kick meant to sweep his legs out from beneath him and came up against a wall of muscle instead. He didn't try to deflect me. His hard legs bruised mine and sent me backward reflexively without him having to budge an inch.

Goddess, this is bad, I thought, executing a throw meant to hit a pressure point.

That one he caught, his meaty hand snatching my wrist and twisting hard until it popped.

I bit my lip to hold back my yelp.

But I couldn't hide my flinch.

Or the shudder of pain that shot up my arm.

I still had two more moves to execute, and I was pretty sure he'd sprained my wrist.

Sweat beaded down my spine. Giving up wasn't an option. I couldn't fail again.

So I feigned a movement toward his groin with my knee, then threw my elbow upward at the last second in a move similar to what Master Cedric had shown yesterday.

I caught the giant in the chin and followed it up with a final chop to his neck.

It barely fazed him, his brown eyes blinking at me with that perpetual boredom. Like I was merely a fly buzzing around his head.

"Switch," Master Cedric said, his command lighting a fire in my partner's gaze. He struck out with the force of a lightning bolt, going for my neck. I ducked on instinct, using my smaller frame to my advantage.

His elbow knocked the back of my head, shooting an agonizing spike down my neck. But I moved with it and out to the side, just to see his heel coming up toward my nose.

I leapt backward, barely missing his kick.

He followed me, his steps athletic and lithe. His face gave nothing away, his emotionless state making my blood thrum harshly through my veins.

I couldn't remember how many moves he'd attempted already, just kept hearing Master Cedric's earlier instructions.

"You are welcome to execute more than four moves on the offensive as well. Four is the minimum."

He hadn't let me try more than four.

He'd told us to switch.

How many would he allow my partner to do? Would Master Cedric stop this prospect at four or wait until the man destroyed me?

He'd asked me last night if I remembered what happened if I disobeyed him.

You'll fail me.

I'd thought he'd intended to punish me then.

But he hadn't.

Maybe this was the real punishment, my true failure, my *death*.

My breath caught in my throat as I dodged another hit, then I rolled to escape his foot again. But he was coming faster now, his movements harsh and strong and *deadly*.

Master Cedric said nothing.

The room was silent apart from my harsh inhales and exhales.

He wasn't going to stop this.

And my partner seemed hell-bent on proving his mastery by using me as his punching bag.

I couldn't run. I couldn't hide. I had to fight.

But I was no match for his size and power. Even if I found a way to punch him, it wouldn't do much. Without a weapon, I was fucked.

My wrist was on fire from whatever he'd done to it.

Tears threatened my vision, true fear strangling my throat.

Please call it, I thought, begging Master Cedric with my mind. *Please don't let me fail like this. Not after everything I've—*

Prospect Six Hundred and Forty-Two caught my wounded wrist and tugged me within reach, then twisted it sharply to snap the bones in my arm.

It happened so suddenly that I barely processed it, could hardly feel the agony until his knee slammed into my stomach and his elbow hit my head.

The world spun, my back hitting the mat with a whoosh of sound that expelled all my air.

He started to fall down on top of me, his face swimming in my vision. But a harsh command from Master Cedric paused the movement.

Or maybe that was a dream.

I couldn't really see. Couldn't truly process. Everything was blurry. Dark, then bright.

Ohh, this hurts, I thought, doing my best not to make a sound. But a tiny moan escaped me. All my training to *endure* snapped into focus as I tried with all my might to rein in the agony, to persevere despite the weight holding me down.

Move, I commanded myself. *Get. Up. And. Move.*

My vision failed me as I tried to find my way off the mat. Half my body seemed incapable of moving. *He broke my arm.* That hit to my head had knocked me off-kilter. My stomach felt twisted inside out.

I stole a shallow breath and closed my eyes.

Three. Two. Now.

I gritted my teeth and rolled, then forced my knees to tuck underneath me and used my good hand to push myself up off the mat. I still couldn't really see or hear, but I sensed everyone watching my struggle.

This was my battle to fight. My battle to *win*.

Just as Six had survived his punishment, I would persevere through mine.

There was no alternative.

I wanted to live.

And I proved it by finding my footing and hobbling to the wall beside the beastly male.

"Prospect One Hundred and Thirty-Nine, you're up," Master Cedric said in a bored tone, calling my former sparring partner to the mat.

I tried to watch her fight, but my vision continued to blink in and out of focus. I wasn't sure how many movements she executed, but I heard the distinctive crunch of bone when the male went next.

Her agonized shriek pierced the air, telling me he'd done severe damage.

But then she went quiet.

I wasn't sure if that was a result of her training or if she'd fallen unconscious.

Another smack followed.

Another crunch.

"Next," Master Cedric said, his tone dismissive. "And please deposit Prospect One Hundred and Thirty-Nine in the hallway."

"Yes, Master Cedric," the male replied without emotion.

She's dead, I realized, still unable to see. *Or she's about to die.*

That'd be the only reason to take her into the hall.

My insides churned at the realization that he'd let this happen, that he'd let that human kill her.

But of course he had.

That was how this entire program worked. Only the strongest survived. And he'd just given me the ultimate lesson.

Providing proof of what he'd been trying to tell me through each failure.

You don't have what it takes to pass this course.

He hadn't actually said that. However, he didn't need to.

Because I understood why he kept failing me now.

I wasn't strong enough to handle this.

Which meant I could never be a Vigil.

So what would become of me now? Would I even survive long enough to attend my Blood Day?

Not with Master Cedric's course haunting my life.

I should never have enrolled in combat training.

But there wasn't anything I could do about it now.

Just endure it.

And try to find a way to survive.

CEDRIC

Lily's ashen features haunted the edge of my peripheral vision. She did her best to remain upright against the wall while everyone executed today's assignment on the mats. However, I could taste her pain on my tongue.

I'd almost dismissed her to the hallway to join her former partner, but the notion of sending her off with the medics didn't sit well with me.

The other prospect would live, assuming the medical staff decided her test scores marked her as worthy enough for recovery.

Given how poorly I'd graded Lily in my class, her injuries might be overlooked or left to fester.

It was a risk I refused to take.

So I forced her to stay despite knowing she was suffering horribly inside. It was a testament to her inner strength that she managed to remain standing.

By the time the final prospects stepped up to the mat, my patience had hit an all-time low. So I only allowed them four moves each before I dismissed the class.

I nearly called for Lily to remain behind, but I caught

her determined movements from the corner of my eye and decided to see what she had in mind first.

Everyone left quickly, none of them noticing or caring about her slow movements.

That was how this new world worked.

Because the vampires and lycans in charge had devised a mechanism that pitted humans against each other, making them compete for the chance of becoming an immortal, all to the detriment of their former camaraderie.

It hadn't always been this way.

Mortals used to work together, or at least seek companionship from one another.

But not now.

Now they didn't even care that Lily was likely going to die from her internal injuries. None of them searched for the other prospect either, her life already forgotten.

What I'd done today was cruel, but that didn't belittle its importance.

Lily needed to understand that her pursuit of a Vigil existence would never come to fruition. Humans fought against each other now. There was no mercy. And her petite size made her an easy target, one her fellow mortals would use against her without a second thought.

Her partner tonight had beaten the shit out of her without batting an eye.

And the other female's sparring mate had been even worse.

This wasn't the existence she truly desired.

Something she now knew, thanks to tonight's lesson.

I'd expected her to grab her bag and leave with the others, heading back to her room with the hopes of maybe requesting a schedule change.

I wouldn't have allowed her to get that far.

But that'd been my expectation after her failure tonight.

Instead, she surprised me by staying behind and heading over to her mat.

Where she proceeded to pull off her pants with one hand—something she clearly struggled to do.

And then she began the painstaking process of removing her shirt with a broken arm.

Her hiss of pain was quickly swallowed, her determination momentarily striking me speechless.

Then she slowly went to her knees in a submissive pose.

I gaped at her, stunned by her obedience and determination. That couldn't have been easy for her—something she confirmed as a violent shudder nearly sent her sideways to the mat. But her muscles locked, and she closed her eyes as she gritted her teeth through the pain.

"If I told you to repeat the fight sequence right now, you'd do it, wouldn't you?" I voiced the thought out loud because I was stunned by her kneeling form.

Rather than reply, she stole a deep breath and started to stand. When her feet went into the fighting stance, I darted forward to grab her hips and stop her.

"It wasn't a request or a demand," I said, my voice colder than I'd intended. But I was pissed that she'd almost begun the routine—a routine that would surely damage her more because it would require sharp movements with her fractured arm.

Her body trembled against mine, her bottom lip disappearing between her teeth.

A coppery scent filled the air in the next moment, the fragrance drawing my focus to her mouth. She was trying to mask her pain because that was what she'd been taught. And in doing so, she'd bitten her lip so hard that it bled.

I wrapped an arm around her waist to hold her against

me and used my free hand to tug her lip free. She flinched, her eyes going unfocused for a second, then she blinked repeatedly as though trying to stay awake.

The injury to her head was worse than I'd suspected. I could see the agony in her dilated pupils and hear the internal damage to her abdomen and lungs through her raspy breaths.

"My delicate little flower," I murmured, leaning down to lick the blood from her lip. She shivered, her reaction vibrating every inch of me. "Are you strong enough to put your clothes back on?"

She swallowed. "Y-yes."

She didn't sound very sure. Actually, she sounded almost mortified by the request. Maybe because it'd taken so much effort to undress. "Try for me," I said, my tongue tracing her lip again to steal the fresh trickle of blood. "I need to send a message, then we'll go."

I didn't elaborate on where or what I meant. Instead, I gently released her, but my hands hovered nearby in case she started to fall again.

She swayed a little, her eyes squinting closed for a long beat.

I waited.

Then she blew out a breath and righted herself.

When her eyes opened, they went a little wide at seeing me still right in front of her. Then she turned toward her clothes and showed me the redness forming on her back.

She'd hit that mat hard.

Her balance shifted as she tried to bend and pick up her pants, her knees giving out beneath her.

I caught her again, this time lifting her into the air and carrying her to my desk. I didn't bother chastising her for her inability to dress herself. She'd tried and she was in pain.

Because of my lesson, I thought darkly.

She swayed a little as I set her on the wood surface, her gaze seeming to go in and out of focus. "Do you know why I changed your partner in tonight's class?" I asked her.

She started to nod, then stopped to swallow, another of those convulsions going through her. "To show me I'm too weak for this."

I frowned, not liking the way that sounded. "No. I wanted you to understand that perfect form means nothing against someone twice your size."

I didn't like to think of her as *weak*, just delicate. Which wasn't her fault.

This society had ensured that she remained petite.

She was strong for her size, and her determination was admirable, but she couldn't win against someone like Prospect Six Hundred and Forty-Two. It was a simple matter of size and strength.

But that didn't make her weak.

"Strength isn't always physical," I told her softly before going to retrieve her clothes.

She remained silent as I started dressing her. I worked on her pants first, noting the bruises forming on her legs from trying to kick her partner tonight. It distracted me from admiring the apex between her thighs, my focus too consumed by the blemishes on her skin.

Just as the sunken quality of her abdomen and the bruising along her ribs kept me from enjoying the sight of her full breasts.

She had to be in unspeakable pain.

Which again was my fault for allowing tonight's lesson to occur.

I wouldn't take it back.

She needed to understand how this world worked.

It was a distinction I shouldn't be trying to teach her, as

her life would end soon regardless of that knowledge, but I felt compelled to help her in this small way.

Sighing, I tugged the white cotton over her head and then carefully guided her upper limbs through the arms of the shirt. She remained silent while I worked, only slightly flinching when I touched her wounded wrist and forearm.

Definitely broken, I thought, noting the swelling spiraling from her wrist up to her elbow.

It would take her months to heal from these injuries.

And that was only if the medics allowed it.

Grinding my teeth, I stepped away from her to retrieve my tablet from the desk.

I didn't even really think about my plans; I just selected her name in the Blood University records and opened the off-site assignment form.

Submitting it would allow me to take her off the university grounds for a day.

No one would question the request, as the staff here often borrowed humans for personal reasons. Some wanted a temporary maid for a day. Others wanted a fuck toy or a blood bag or both.

It didn't matter.

Taking a student for a test-drive was considered to be one of the few perks of working at Blood University.

It was something I'd never done.

But I'd only been instructing this course for a few years.

Before that, I'd been playing in Silvano's political games.

This was my sabbatical.

Or escape, really.

And now I had a human pet to play with for the next twenty-four hours.

Under "Reason for off-site assignment," I wrote *physical training*.

Then I hit Send and went to retrieve my shoulder bag from the closet. I slipped my tablet inside and picked up Lily's bag and her shoes on my way back to her.

She still had that unfocused look about her, making me wonder if she even noticed my movements as I slid the socks and shoes onto her feet.

"Can you walk?" I asked when I finished.

She tried to nod and almost fell in the process, causing me to snort.

"I didn't think so." She'd expended the last of her strength by trying to placate me with her submission on the mat.

Shifting the bags to one arm, I used my opposite to lift her off the desk, then situated her into a cradle-like position against my chest.

"Close your eyes and try not to scream," I told her. "This may hurt a little."

I didn't often phase while holding others, and I wasn't sure how the abrupt movement would impact her injuries.

She clung to my dress shirt as I engaged my ability, taking us from the classroom to the parking lot in a literal blink of an eye.

Teleportation was a unique ability among my kind, often only adapted through certain bloodlines and perfected with age. I was the only vampire at the university here with the skill, which explained Lily's wide eyes as she gaped at our new surroundings.

Rather than explain, I used my foot to wake up the sensor beneath my car. The door of my two-seater coupe hissed open in an upward angle to reveal the bucket seat inside.

I set Lily on the leather and tossed our bags into the small area by her feet. She trembled, clearly uncertain about my intentions. But she didn't speak.

I guided the belt across her to buckle her in, as I suspected she'd never been in a car before. There weren't any excursions on her record, which meant she'd never left the university grounds. And driving training wasn't an offered course.

I shut the door.

Walked around the car.

And settled beside her.

"Ready to go for a ride, darling?" I asked as the engine roared to life before us.

She swallowed, her big blue-green eyes glancing at me with a mixture of fear and intrigue.

I studied her for a moment, my gaze falling to her puffy lip before meeting her eyes once more. "A weak human wouldn't even be conscious right now, Lily."

Her brow crinkled at my nickname for her.

But I didn't explain it.

Instead, I lifted my hand to gently cup her cheek. "Tonight was a demonstration of how perfect technique can fail you, not a lesson in weakness." I drew my thumb along her lower lip. "Now I'm going to show you what it feels like to be strong."

By giving her something I shouldn't.

And revealing a secret that could cost us both her life.

But there was no other choice.

Either I did this and she survived…

Or I did nothing and she died.

I wasn't ready for her to wilt just yet.

So instead, I'd help her blossom once more.

Into a new kind of flower—one infused by immortal blood.

LILY

Master Cedric can teleport.

I'm in a car.

Master Cedric said I'm not weak.

The thoughts spun through my mind in various sequences, my brain struggling to string logic to each one.

When he'd lifted me into his arms, I hadn't known what to expect. Then he'd told me to close my eyes and try not to scream.

Before *teleporting* us out of the classroom and into a car park.

I didn't even know this part of the university existed, as it was outside the walls.

Walls he'd phased through to reach his car.

A car I was now sitting in.

I'd never ridden in an automobile before. Nor had I ever teleported before. I hadn't even known the latter was possible. I could still feel the wind on my face and the churning in my stomach from moving impossibly fast.

Or maybe that was the residual ache from being beaten up by Prospect Six Hundred and Forty-Two.

I'd thought the purpose was to demonstrate my weakness.

But Master Cedric had said it was to show me how perfect technique didn't matter against someone twice my size.

And now we were driving into the night on a sleek black road surrounded by desert.

Where are you taking me? I wanted to ask.

However, I remained silent. I knew better than to question a superior.

Except I was likely going to die soon. If not from my injuries tonight, then from a future class. Because there was no way I could heal properly before my next sparring session. Which meant my time here was limited.

So what would it hurt to voice my inquiry?

Maybe Master Cedric would accelerate my fate.

Given how I felt right now, that might not be a bad thing.

"Where are we going?" I asked before I could change my mind. Not the most intelligent decision on my part, but I felt oddly emboldened by sharing my thoughts. It made me want to do it again.

"To my temporary home," he replied, surprising me.

"Temporary home?" I repeated, my brow furrowing.

He glanced at me, his lips curling. "Feeling chatty, darling? Perhaps you're not as wounded as I thought." His gaze fell to my arm before returning his focus to the road. "Or maybe you hit your head against the mat harder than I realized."

I frowned. I didn't remember hitting my head. But that sounded right.

Every part of me ached, from my head down to my shins.

"It's temporary because I don't plan to stay long," he explained, surprising me again with his answer.

It wasn't my right to ask questions, yet he'd responded as though he didn't mind at all that I'd requested clarification.

"I only accepted the role here to avoid a political request," he went on. "All of the other staff here have their own homes in the desert because they don't really have a choice otherwise. It's that or remain at the university with the students, which a handful of lower-ranking lycans already do for security reasons."

Yes, that I knew. Well, not the lower-ranking part. But I had a lycan headmaster in my dormitory. I avoided her when I could, as she often tormented those who crossed her path. She struck me as angry. *Very* angry.

"I was given a choice of building a home or accepting royal accommodations," he continued. "I opted for the latter because, as I said, I don't intend to remain long-term. And the royals don't often visit, which keeps the palace quiet."

Royal accommodations? I'd never heard of that. I also didn't realize that our Masters left the university grounds. No one had ever explained that part to us, as it wasn't our business to know.

Yet Master Cedric seemed to be in a sharing mood.

Maybe because he was planning to kill me and didn't see any harm in revealing these details.

Or he wasn't planning to kill me but knew my time here was limited.

"While I understand the purpose of having a royal palace near each Blood University, it does seem rather wasteful since no one ever visits these areas," he added, distracting me from my thoughts. "But I'm putting this one to good use, at least for now."

I blinked at him. "There's a royal palace? For… for the…?" I couldn't finish the comment.

I knew who the royals were. The purpose of my politics course was to learn more about the lineages of all the royal vampires and alpha lycans. They were the rulers of the world, each of them assigned to their own regions where they governed and ruled the lands around them.

"It's a palace meant to house visiting royals or alphas who want to check in on the local Blood University," he said, answering my question again. "In the early days, they stopped by often. Now, most of those estates are abandoned. Except for the staff, anyway."

Master Cedric turned onto a new road, this one just as dark as the former one, his headlights the only source of brightness around us.

"It seemed like a waste of resources to build a home I don't intend to keep." He shrugged. "So I took advantage of my hierarchy in Silvano's bloodline and accepted a room at the palace instead."

My eyes widened. "Prince Silvano…" I knew his name and face from my classes. He had cruel black eyes, similar to Master Cedric's. But the royal vampire's hair was a shock of white strands, not dark like Master Cedric's hair.

"Yes, my Sire," Master Cedric replied, his bored tone belying the importance of what he'd just revealed.

Prince Silvano was a powerful vampire.

A royal. One of the oldest of vampire kind.

And if Master Cedric was his progeny, that marked him as extremely high in the vampire hierarchy.

"I only accepted the role here to avoid a political request."

That comment took on a whole new meaning.

He could be eligible for a sovereign position with his bloodline link.

Which marked him as extremely powerful.

And I'm in a car alone with him.

"Hmm," he hummed, his nostrils flaring. "Your fear is seducing my inner predator, little flower."

His quiet tone just made those words more threatening.

"Breathe for me," he whispered. "Inhale slowly and then exhale."

I swallowed, only then noticing the burn in my chest. Because I'd stopped breathing upon the reveal of his royal lineage.

My lungs refused to operate, my mind incapable of controlling my body.

I couldn't remember how to inhale.

Master Cedric's palm went to my thigh, giving it a squeeze. "Now, Lily."

I gasped, at both his tone and his touch. Warmth spread from his hand up my leg to my abdomen, making it clench as my lungs expanded with more air.

"Good girl," he murmured, his thumb stroking the inside of my thigh. "Keep breathing for me, sweet flower. I'll fix you soon."

My brow came down. *Fix me?*

"But if you utter a word to anyone about any of this, you'll die." His grip tightened a little, something I didn't need because the warning in his voice was clear enough.

"I won't." My reply left me on a wheeze, my lungs demanding more oxygen. But I couldn't seem to pull in enough, my side aching with the effort.

His words had left me speechless, my emotions choking me entirely. However, this issue seemed related to my stomach more than my fear of him and what he intended to do.

I felt so light-headed.

My vision kept blinking in and out like it had during class.

"Ask me what political position I'm avoiding," he told me.

I opened my mouth to voice the words, but they seemed too long. I didn't have enough air. So I went with a guess instead. "Sovereign."

His thumb did a little circle against my leg. "Your political marks are well earned, little flower." He gave me another squeeze before releasing me to handle the wheel. The car moved around us, turning again.

Only this time, I couldn't see the new road.

My vision had blacked out completely.

"Almost there," Master Cedric said, his voice sounding far away. "Keep breathing, Lily."

I did.

Barely.

By the time the car stopped, I felt like I was floating off in a cloud of nothingness. I vaguely sensed lights around us. My nose picked up on a woodsy scent of some kind. Then salt. A hum of sound. Strong arms lifting me from the car.

It all blurred together.

Until I landed on a true cloud of softness. Warmth. Engulfing me from head to toe.

Ohhh... I almost moaned, my skin reveling in the silky texture.

If this was the afterlife, I accepted it.

"Shh." The hush against my ear was accompanied by the heat of a hard, hot male slipping into the cloud behind me. "Keep moaning and rolling around like that, and my plans for you are going to change."

Master Cedric.

I tried to open my eyes to see what he was doing, to determine where we were, but everything remained hidden in a sea of darkness. His minty scent swirled around me, suffocating me beneath the intensity of his presence.

"Drink, little flower." The words were accompanied by something warm and wet against my mouth. I parted my lips in response, trying to follow his command.

Something sticky and sweet touched my tongue, the taste causing my nostrils to flare and my thighs to squeeze. *Oh, Goddess...* I didn't know what this was, but it was decadent and overwhelming.

"Seal your mouth around it and suck," he whispered.

I did what he told me to do, filling my mouth with ambrosia and drowning myself in it.

"Swallow," he added, his voice deep and sensual.

My heart raced in my chest as I complied. Heat spread through me, causing me to wince as it reached my tender arm. The pain had dulled to a residual ache I'd been able to ignore, thanks to the overpowering agony in my stomach, but it roared back to life with a vengeance.

"Keep sucking and swallowing," Master Cedric demanded, his voice rumbling through me and forcing me to obey.

It hurt.

It tasted so good.

It burned.

Oh, but I wanted to make a meal of this liquid and never drink anything else again.

Such a conflict of sensation, both hot and agonizing. A sensually lethal mix of reactions that rendered me compliant against him.

I just kept sucking and swallowing, causing a torturous inferno to grow inside me. My limbs shook, shooting agony back to my heart and up my spine. I pushed it back, trying my hardest not to let any of my pain show, but it exploded from me in a hot wave of torment that left my mouth on a screaming gurgle.

Master Cedric silenced me by placing that liquid against my lips again. "Just a little more, then I'll put you to sleep."

I wasn't sure what that meant.

But I tried to obey anyway.

What choice did I have?

His body was wrapped around mine, his arm clamped around me, and his hand...

My brow crinkled.

His wrist... that's what he keeps pressing to my mouth.

My eyes flew open, my sight returning in an instant and stirring sharp spikes around my temple. We were in a bed decorated in black linen with a wall of windows overlooking the darkness outside.

The lighting in the room was low, reminding me of flickering candles.

And there was dark wood furniture beside us. *A nightstand.*

Another bolt ricocheted down my spine, drawing a gasp from my throat.

I sputtered and choked on his blood in response, then swallowed as it came back up. Master Cedric's lips brushed my temple, his wrist leaving my mouth. His fingers whispered across my throat to my shoulder and then down my injured arm.

I bit my lip to keep from shrieking as he slowly extended it. "This will help it mend," he told me softly, his mouth still against my temple. "I'll hold you while you rest, Lily. And tomorrow you'll feel invincible."

I wasn't so sure about that.

I felt like death.

Broken.

Unable to speak.

Suffocating on his blood.

Why did he do that? Why make me drink from him? Vampires drank from humans, not the other way around.

Had he wanted to taunt me with his ambrosia-like taste before I died?

Because I could still feel his essence warming my insides, his blood an elixir unlike any I'd ever experienced.

"Sleep." The word a breath against my ear, making my eyelids droop. It was an instant reaction, my body succumbing to his demand as though he owned me.

And maybe he did.

Maybe this was my end.

I wanted to fight it, to beg for another chance, but my mouth refused me. My body was already falling into the cloud of black silk, bending to his demand.

His mouth brushed my throat, his tongue circling my pulse.

This was it.

My end.

The final moments of my life.

"Good night, little flower." His voice followed me into the darkness, his final words that repeated through my thoughts until nothing else existed.

Only darkness.

And... *peace.*

CEDRIC

I dabbed Lily's chin with a wet washcloth, cleaning the blood off her skin.

My little flower had wilted so quickly on the drive, talking to me one moment and incoherent the next.

I'd worried I would have to force-feed her, which I'd done to an extent. But she'd returned long enough to swallow on her own. And now her body would take care of the rest.

She'd imbibed more than enough of my essence to thrive. It would have some residual effects for a few days, too.

So I'd need to find a reason to excuse her from her courses.

Otherwise, her enhancement would be obvious to those around her.

I also needed to ensure she understood the importance of what I'd done and why she couldn't tell a soul. She'd already agreed to it in the car, but her response had felt more programmed than true. I would take the next few days to make sure she truly meant her compliance for the right reasons.

"There," I murmured, studying her pretty face. "Good as new."

I set the cloth to the side and focused on her arm again, straightening it once more to ensure the bones settled appropriately. Sometimes enhanced healing caused the bones to set at an awkward angle, which resulted in having to break them again to mend them properly. I also pulled her legs down and rolled her to her back, wanting her organs and insides to repair themselves without issue as well.

It shouldn't take long.

Her injuries were substantial and would have been life-threatening if left unattended, but my blood would cure her in a few hours.

Still, I remained beside her in the bed while she healed, just in case something went wrong. She rested beautifully on her back, her pretty blonde hair fanned out around her head.

I let her steady pulse soothe my nerves while I worked on my tablet. I had several messages to reply to, including one from Silvano.

It ended in the same way all his messages did. *When will you be back?*

"Never, if I can help it," I muttered out loud. But I couldn't reply that way.

Fortunately, there weren't cameras in this house—something I'd checked upon moving in and regularly scanned for while living here.

Lilith favored technology, using it as a way to keep not only humans in line, but her lycans and her own kind as well.

I would never understand how the royals decided on her leadership. She wasn't even the oldest vampire among us. Kylan owned that role, followed closely by Jace.

Well, technically, *Cam* was the oldest.

But he was presumed dead.

So that left Kylan.

Even Silvano was older than Lilith.

Not that he should ever lead. He was a sadist with a power complex, hence the reason I chose to hide in the middle of the fucking desert.

Many assumed we shared similar proclivities since he'd sired me, but I preferred consenting prey. I glanced down at the blonde behind me. "Hmm, maybe I like wilting flowers, too," I mused aloud.

Wilting flowers with spirit.

When Lily had questioned me in the car, I'd been thrilled. That was why I'd divulged so much information to her afterward. It had taken courage on her part to ask such a question. And it was a simple one, too. The kind of question a human would have asked with ease two centuries ago.

But not now.

Now they barely even looked at supernaturals, let alone spoke freely to them.

But my Lily had shown a hint of strength beneath all those submissive layers, and I intended to start coaxing that part of her out to play.

A dangerous desire, considering her future. Alas, that was a problem we'd address in time.

For now, I'd help her blossom and enjoy the short time she had left on this earth.

I ran my fingers through her silky blonde hair, then worked on my reply to Silvano. I suggested we meet at the next Blood Day to discuss it, which was a little under nine months away. That would give me time to finish out my course regimen for the year and also create a new excuse for avoiding his request.

His increased pestering of late told me I was running out of time. He'd want a formal response to his political request soon.

Which meant I'd probably end up a sovereign in the next few years.

Because no one denied Silvano and survived it.

I didn't mind the position or the responsibility that came with it, but I didn't want to be under my Sire's thumb more than I already was. He'd turned me over three thousand years ago, and we'd ventured in separate directions ever since.

We both adored blood and violence.

But I preferred a physical fight, while he enjoyed torture. It had allowed us to be a powerful duo once. However, his sanity of late felt a bit lacking.

He loved this new world order, enjoyed taking out his superiority on the humans and forcing them to bow at his feet.

I found it all a bit droll.

There were benefits.

And there were negatives.

Such as the beauty lying beside me.

She should be in a field somewhere, picking flowers and lazing in the sun. Not attending a university meant to indoctrinate mortal slaves.

"You definitely shouldn't be in my class," I added aloud, my fingers returning to her hair. "My course is all about murder and darkness, and you're life and light personified." I studied her delicate features once more, then checked on her arm again.

The Blood University had practically starved her, which was part of what made her so fragile.

I had no doubt she could be a fighter, if that was what she truly desired in life. But not under these circumstances.

Harming her in class tonight had been more difficult than I'd anticipated. I'd nearly killed her partner for laying a hand on her. Which was partly why I'd allowed the female to be so badly injured in the next round—I'd been distracted by my own murderous rage.

Then I'd chastised myself for setting up the failure.

But she needed to understand that perfect form meant nothing against someone twice her size.

"Maybe I'll show you how to use other means to your advantage," I told her as I drew my touch up her sternum to her neck. "I bet you would be handy with a blade."

Although, Vigils weren't given weapons often. Only the most trusted among them were given machine guns.

Which required muscle and size.

And at least a decade of training within the Vigil unit.

She'd never survive that. Not with the way this world had stacked its cards against her.

"I should have let you die tonight," I confided out loud. "Expedited the process by drinking you dry." It was a notion that had crossed my mind. But I'd killed it almost immediately. "I'm not ready for you to wilt yet. Which I suppose makes me a selfish bastard, but it's been a long time since something has intrigued me like you do, Lily."

It was probably just a result of boredom.

This new world took the surprise and excitement out of every situation.

"I didn't understand why you enrolled in my course," I continued, aware that she couldn't hear me at all. But I felt like talking to her, so I did. "I immediately pulled up your records and saw they were almost flawless, so it became apparent to me that you were one of the many humans attempting to qualify for the Immortal Cup."

I checked my email once more, noted that I'd gone

through enough for the day, and set the tablet aside so I could lie down beside her in the bed.

I'd already lost my shirt and shoes when I'd grabbed the washcloth earlier, and I'd swapped my dress pants for a pair of sweats. But I'd left Lily in her clothes, unsure of how she preferred to sleep.

She was still on her back, her beautiful body healing.

I went to my side, propping my head up on my hand and placing my opposite palm on her stomach. Then I pulled up her shirt to study her creamy skin. The initial signs of bruising had disappeared, confirming my blood was doing its job.

I drew my thumb around her belly button, sighing. "It's true that scores can help you qualify for the Immortal Cup. But genetics play a large part in it as well. And your genetics mark you as ideal for a harem. You're beautiful and petite, and I imagine your advisor—if that term is even accurate—is pushing you toward sexual arts classes. That's likely why you've taken two in the last year."

It would also have something to do with her age.

But the powers that be would want to know how she performed sexually to confirm their harem assessment.

"Prospects are preselected for the Immortal Cup. Sometimes a prospect with insanely high scores can qualify as a replacement, but it's not what you think. None of it is. They choose nearly three dozen, then immediately cut the numbers by allowing each royal and each alpha to pick one candidate for their harem. Then only twelve go on to compete."

That competition was then televised for all the mortals to see.

Giving them all a false hope of a future they could attain if they just worked harder.

And it seduced humans like my Lily to kill herself trying to become an immortal.

"It's a sadistic system meant to break the spirits of your kind," I added softly, my knuckles brushing her flat abdomen. "I'm sorry, Lily. If I could help you pursue this path, I would. But you were destined to fail before you even began."

I leaned down to brush a kiss against her forehead.

Then I sighed again—a sound I seemed to make a lot in her presence—and settled into my pillow. "We'll discuss more when you wake," I said, my palm flattening against her abdomen.

I couldn't remember the last time I'd had another person in my bed.

A century or two ago, maybe?

Silvano often gifted me his used-up harem members, but I didn't fuck them. I fed them and left them to heal in a guest room instead.

It just wasn't all that appealing to me to have his leftovers.

There were only two that I'd killed just to put them out of their misery. They were going to die anyway, and their lifeless eyes had seemed to beg me to do it.

Unlike Lily.

She was so full of life and determination, even when she'd started to fall asleep in my arms tonight. I'd felt her desire to live like a push against my conscience.

It'd been refreshing and made my gift to her all the more worth it.

Maybe I could find a way to keep her.

Of course, that would set her in Silvano's sights.

So perhaps not.

However, she was mine for the moment.

That would just have to be long enough.

I ran my hands over her one more time, checking her injuries and noting the healing marks on her body. Her arm was almost fully mended, thus allowing me to move her again.

I curled her into a similar position as before, with her back to my front, but I didn't press my wrist to her lips. Instead, I wrapped myself around her and guided her head to my upper arm to use as a pillow while my opposite arm went around her stomach.

Mine, I thought, using my body to shield her from the world.

I pressed my nose to her hair and inhaled her floral scent.

My sweet flower.

My Lily.

For tonight, you are simply mine.

LILY

Everything tingled.

My toes.

My fingers.

My eyelashes.

Such a strange sensation, like I could feel every inch of my body, even the hairs along my neck.

I felt *alive*.

There were sounds all around me, scents that overwhelmed my senses, and tastes that layered my tongue in forbidden desires.

Is this death? I wondered. How cruel would it be to feel so incredibly refreshed just to realize I'd joined the afterlife?

Oh, but if it felt like this, then I welcomed this change.

Every part of me hummed with electricity, my body on fire with sensation.

Heat bathed my back and wrapped around my torso. *Masculine heat.*

I inhaled, indulging in the minty scent. It was so heavy and intoxicating.

Master Cedric.

It felt like a dream waking up in his arms. But he was behind me. I could sense him as though he were part of me. I blinked, an array of colors piercing my vision as the room came into view.

Rich browns and blacks and a window revealing a courtyard of trees and fountains beneath a moon. I gasped at it, the lush greenery unlike anything I'd ever seen.

It didn't look real.

It was too defined. Too bright. Too *vibrant*.

Master Cedric's thumb shifted along my skin, drawing my focus to the palm against my abdomen.

Beneath my shirt.

That shouldn't shock me. But somehow it felt so incredibly intimate. Like a brand.

Heat radiated from his palm, claiming my skin with little hot fibers that stroked my nerve endings.

It was intense. Amazing. The most intimate touch of my life.

Which made no sense.

I'd been naked and stroked all over my body.

But that hand felt brand new. Like I was being caressed for the first time.

And the heat at my back resembled the desert sun, just without the squelching dehydration that came with it. Instead, it left me feeling rejuvenated by fire.

His thumb moved again, the slight caress making me shiver all the way to my core. It was so *hot* and intense and overwhelming and *new*.

"Mmm, you're awake."

Was his voice always this melodic? Or is this new?

"How do you feel, little flower?"

So deep and powerful, I thought, squirming a little.

Which was precisely the wrong thing to do. Because one clench of my thighs had me jolting back against him.

A moan escaped my lips in response, my entire body erupting in flames.

"That good, hmm?" He chuckled, the vibration causing my nipples to stiffen painfully beneath my shirt.

"What's happening to me?" I asked, my voice breathier than I'd expected.

"I believe you're aroused," he whispered, his palm gliding upward to stroke the underside of my breast.

I arched back into him, reacting to his touch and seeking more. "Everything is so potent," I marveled, the room spinning with vibrant color as my skin prickled from his heat. "I… I feel… *alive*."

"Because you are, little flower." He kissed the back of my head, his hand skimming upward to cup my breast. "You're feeling the effects of my blood."

That sentence should have given me pause and forced me to consider my situation, but his thumb brushed my nipple in the next instant, causing my mind to fracture beneath a wave of intense sensation.

"So sensitive," he murmured, his touch sending a hum of electricity through my limbs.

My legs tensed in response, and that fire within grew. "Master Cedric," I breathed, uncertain of what I wanted him to do or why I was even saying his name. But I felt like I was going to explode, and I wasn't sure if that was good or bad.

"Just 'Cedric' will do." His lips were at my ear. "Formalities are for school, not for my bedroom."

I couldn't fathom a reply, not with his hand on my breast and his touch circling my stiff peak.

He pinched it between his finger and thumb, eliciting a guttural sound from my throat. Every part of me trembled, my insides turning to molten lava in reaction to his touch.

No one had ever made me feel like this.

Not that my experience was vast. I'd only taken one and a half courses, and the focus had been more on pleasing the males than anything else.

That was probably why Six kept losing. His mouth on my body did nothing for me.

But Master Cedric's hand absolutely did.

"You're trembling." His words were quiet against my ear, his lips warm and soft. He swept his thumb across my sensitive tip again, then slid his palm back to my abdomen. "Everything feels more intense and powerful for you right now, doesn't it? You can't even remember the pain from your arm at all anymore, can you?"

My reply was unintelligible because I seemed to have forgotten how to speak.

His hand was still moving.

Going to the waistband of my pants.

And slipping beneath the fabric.

I froze against him, terrified and captivated by what he intended to do. How it would feel. How my body would react.

His breath teased my ear, his hard body holding mine as his fingers brushed my shaved mound.

My next grooming appointment was later this week, so I knew I was a little prickly down there.

But he didn't comment.

Instead, he licked the outer shell of my ear as his hand cupped me between my thighs.

I nearly flew off the bed, his skin so hot and smooth that I almost couldn't handle his touch.

He hushed me, only then making me realize I'd begun to weep—not in sadness, but in overwhelming pleasure.

I couldn't take it.

It was too much.

And yet I would die if he stopped touching me now.

I didn't recognize myself. I wasn't even sure any of this was real. But I needed him. I... I needed *that.*

A scream left my lips as his fingers explored my damp heat, his touch sliding up to the bundle of nerves and back to my entrance.

"So wet," he praised, his mouth lowering to my throat. "It makes me want to rip off your pants and fuck you into oblivion. But I want to feel you fall apart on my fingers first. Then maybe I'll do it again with my tongue."

Oh, Goddess... I wasn't sure I could survive this. Survive *him.* Not with the wildfire burning inside me, threatening to engulf me from head to toe.

It was so foreign and immense.

So frightening and *hot.*

I swallowed, my body thrumming with this insane urge to burst. Like I was growing and expanding to the point where I would inevitably shatter and never be whole again.

It was all so unfamiliar, so inconceivable, so *good.*

His body held mine with ease, his hand claiming me intimately while his opposite arm cradled my head.

I felt safe. Hot. On the verge of exploding. And utterly overwhelmed by sensation.

It was all too much.

Too bright. Too loud. Too much pressure.

His thumb stoked my need higher and higher, driving me to the precipice of madness.

"Come for me, Lily," he breathed, his words pushing me over the edge into an oblivion of bright stars.

I screamed on my way down, clawing at the air in search of an anchor, a way to pull myself back up into the world.

Only to realize I was still on the bed, reveling in pleasure.

Loudly.

Images of Master Peyton fluttered through my mind, her disapproving glare silencing me in an instant.

She would have bitten my clit for such disobedience.

Then taken me under a wave of orgasms drenched in blood while demanding I remain quiet.

Just like Six.

And that poor boy from—

Master Cedric rolled me to my back, his expression murderous as he glowered down at me.

Goddess, I really messed this up. I parted my lips to apologize, but I couldn't create the right words. It was like my tongue had tied itself in a knot.

"When I make you come, you scream and you don't stop," he told me, his voice holding a lethal edge to it that scattered goose bumps down my spine. "I'm going to please you again, and this time, you're not going to hold back or go silent. You're going to scream my name and enjoy every fucking second."

My lips parted. *He's mad that I stopped screaming?*

"I don't care what the university has taught you, Lily. With me, you will always display your pleasure." His finger penetrated me, stirring a gasp from my throat. "Yes, like that. I want your reactions, little flower. I want to feel you bloom. No silence. No hiding. No torturing yourself with asinine rules when I make you come."

His words rolled across my lips, his mouth having come closer with each statement until his eyes were locked with mine.

But he didn't kiss me. He merely remained right above me as he added a second finger to his penetration below.

A whimper caught in my throat, the pressure almost too much. But then his thumb drifted upward to stroke that sweet spot that made me see stars.

"That's it, sweet flower. Let me see how this feels. Then let me hear it, too."

I swallowed, that bursting sensation building inside me again. I didn't understand why he was doing this or if this was even truly real. But I felt so much. So much heat and intensity. So much anticipation and fear.

Was he warming me up for something nefarious?

Playing with his food before devouring it?

Vampires were notoriously cruel, and Master Cedric had more than lived up to that reputation.

Except he'd fed me.

Given me water.

Taken me in the car.

Fed me his blood.

And now he was watching me with this intense gaze, his dark irises flickering with black flames.

I lost myself in those inky depths, swirling down and around and indulging in the power that was all Master Cedric.

So handsome.

Intimidating.

Dark.

His touch shifted, his fingers working me to exquisite depths as his thumb applied just enough pressure.

It felt like he was pressing on a button, holding it down until the right moment, shifting and petting and prolonging the ecstasy until he desired release.

My release.

An explosion.

A cataclysmic event.

His eyes told me I was right, the male watching me for the exquisite instant of rightness.

"So close," he whispered, his minty breath parting my lips. "You're so very close."

I know, I nearly told him.

"Are you going to scream for me, Lily?"

That nickname rolled off his tongue, going straight to my soul. I'd never been given a name, just a number. And I rather liked the name he'd chosen to call me.

"Are you going to let me feel your release? Make me wish it was my cock inside you instead of my fingers?"

My legs tensed, my mind picturing his crude words with ease. "Please..." I wasn't sure what I wanted. Him to fulfill that fantasy? Him to release my clit? Both?

"Say my name, sweet flower. Ask me to let you come by saying my name."

My mouth went dry, his words and power holding me captive beneath him, dangling on the dangerous edge of climax. "Please, Master—"

He tsked. "Just my name, Lily flower."

I squeezed my eyes shut, the name taunting my tongue.

His teeth sank into my lower lip in response, forcing my eyes wide open again in shock.

"I want to see your pleasure, Lily," he said, his voice holding a touch of reprimand. "And I want to hear you moan my name."

"Cedric." It came out on a hiss-like groan, my veins melting into liquid fire. "Please, Cedric. I need..."

A violent tremble rendered me speechless, his thumb pressing down even harder as his fingers curled inside me. Magic blistered beneath that touch, shooting sparks to each nerve and stirring a garbled plea from my mouth.

Master Cedric bent to kiss me, his tongue soothing the wound he'd made on my lower lip, as his thumb finally released me from my torment.

I screamed into his mouth, the pleasure bordering on pain as it rolled through me with savage vibrations that pierced every inch of my being. My toes curled, my fingers formed fists, and my heart threatened to stop beating.

It stirred another groan from my chest that I couldn't have suppressed even if I wanted to.

And all the while, Master Cedric kissed me, taking in my moans and screams and rewarding my compliance with his tongue.

I felt reborn.

Like he'd just introduced me to a new world of existence.

One that enthralled me and terrified me.

Because this new world felt too real. It felt like the kind of world I could actually enjoy.

And that inspired feelings I didn't want to experience.

Feelings like *hope*.

CEDRIC

"THAT WAS GLORIOUS," I WHISPERED AGAINST HER MOUTH. "Fucking beautiful."

It'd taken a bit of coaxing, mostly because her programming had kicked in midway through her first climax, but the end result was worth the effort.

Her blue-green irises sparkled with residual effects of pleasure, her expression one of wonder and confusion and a hint of fear.

The whole experience proved her sexual training to be lacking, probably because her courses focused more on male pleasure than female enjoyment.

I would fix that.

But she wasn't ready for more right now, something her body confirmed as my thumb brushed her clit. She trembled almost violently in response, her lip disappearing between her teeth as she fought whatever sound threatened to escape.

I slid my hand out from her pants and reached for her chin, using my drenched thumb to tug her lip from her teeth. "Don't hide from me," I told her, my tone lacking in reprimand.

Because I understood her reactions.

She was doing what the university had taught her to do.

However, I wanted her to be real. Whatever that meant. If that was even possible. Maybe it was a fantasy in my mind—the concept of her being true to herself in my presence.

It was certainly a dangerous yearning, one that would inevitably lead to her death.

But at least she would have lived a little before her petals wilted into nothing.

"When we're alone, you can tell me how you feel," I informed her softly. "Be honest, like you were about wanting more training." It'd been so refreshing to see her fight back in her own way, to test the limits of my kindness.

That courage deserved to be rewarded.

It deserved to be cherished and adored and praised.

Not squelched and denied.

I traced her bottom lip with her arousal, allowing the dampness to paint her skin, then I dipped my thumb into her mouth for her to taste. Her pupils dilated, her nostrils flaring. "Do you like that, darling? Do you like the way your pleasure tastes?"

She swallowed, her head dipping a little in confirmation.

"Hmm," I hummed, removing my thumb and leaning in to press my mouth to hers. My tongue licked the residual flavor from her lip before dipping inside to engage her in a sensual kiss underlined in lust. She tentatively returned the embrace, telling me she had never really been kissed before today. I doubted she'd even properly orgasmed, either.

So inexperienced.

Yet perfect in every way.

My delicate, sweet little flower.

I touched my forehead to hers, breathing her in for a long moment, then I dipped one of my fingers into her mouth. "Suck."

She obeyed, her tongue swirling around the tip before taking me deeper.

It was the perfect display of what she would do if this were my cock.

And it made me hard as a fucking rock.

I gave her my other finger, watching as she licked both clean. Then I kissed her, eager to taste more of her arousal. It was an intoxicating blend that set my blood on fire for her.

But the tremble in her shoulders told me she couldn't take much more today.

I wanted her fully aroused and eager to comply, not just acting on duty alone.

Which had been her reaction today. She'd only indulged me because she didn't feel she had a choice. And I supposed she didn't. But that didn't mean she couldn't eventually choose me.

I hadn't actually intended on doing any of this to her today. It'd just been a natural response to her heightened state of senses. Her eyes told me she didn't regret it. The flush on her cheeks told me she'd enjoyed it, too.

I wanted to maintain that enjoyment, not belittle it by pushing her too far.

So instead of demanding that she return the favor, I cupped her cheek and rested my forehead against hers. "I think it's time for a bath." A novelty I doubted she'd ever experienced at the university. I didn't know much about the grooming habits at the school but suspected the showers were communal and supervised by hungry lycans.

"A bath?" she repeated, her alluring irises studying mine.

I smiled. "Yes." It seemed like a suitable way to thank her for her bravery. She might not have interpreted it as such, but she would learn eventually.

Something I could expedite if I kept her here for the remainder of her schooling.

I already had to keep her here for a few days to hide her miraculous recovery, and also to help her ride out the aftereffects of my blood.

"Stay here," I told her.

Not that she had anywhere else to go.

Then I rolled off the bed and ventured into the bathroom to begin pouring a bath. The tub was an indulgence I hadn't really spent much time in, preferring instead to shower quickly.

But it seemed appropriate for Lily.

It would take a while to fill due to the massive size, which was a good thing because I needed a few supplies that weren't in my room.

I left my quarters and ventured into the hallway and searched a few other guest rooms. All of them were equipped with accommodations similar to my own—a large bedroom framed by a walk-out balcony, an adjacent seating area, and two en-suite bathrooms that rivaled the size of most bedrooms.

I finally found what I needed in the fifth set of rooms that I checked. The supplies appeared to be relatively new, suggesting they'd been added recently by one of the staff. There probably hadn't been enough for all the rooms, or maybe they were keeping the extras in storage for future requests from visitors.

I could technically have called one of the staff to the

room to do all this for me, but I preferred to handle my own affairs.

Which was why I rarely interacted with the small group of human servants living on this property. I left the management of their activities to their vampire warden, Adrienne.

She hated her job.

She hated her life.

Mostly because she was no better than a servant here.

She'd not been happy with me moving in, but she'd quickly realized I didn't require much. I barely ate, my age requiring little sustenance to survive.

However, I'd ordered blood products for both of us to keep her from eating the staff—something she'd been doing while maintaining this vacant palace for the last century or so. I imagined it was quite stressful to be in charge of such a space, not knowing when someone might pop in for a visit. It meant she had to keep it meticulously clean and ready, regardless of how many resources that wasted.

And she had a minimal budget to arrange it all.

Hence the reason I'd sponsored the food.

They were all blood slaves whose souls were practically broken from their lives of servitude. Not my favorite flavor. But I had Adrienne turn them into staff over the last few years, thus allowing me to take their blood donations in intervals rather than all at once. It ensured they stayed alive, gave me an endless supply of sustenance, and allowed for more help around the palace.

Positives all around.

I had never understood the point of overindulgence and wasting life, something I'd made very clear to Adrienne when I'd purchased the food stock.

And she'd taken my word as law.

I'd otherwise left her alone, a reaction she seemed grateful for, as she returned the favor in kind.

However, I might need to ask for some additional products to be delivered soon. Like more bath salt.

Assuming I intended to keep Lily here.

It was an idea I pondered on my way back to my room, where I found Lily lying stiff as a board on the bed.

"I said to stay, not to freeze," I told her conversationally on my way to the bathroom. "Why don't you follow me and check out the bath?"

That would give her something to focus on since she seemed to need an order for everything.

Would it be like that if I kept her here? Would she need me to guide her every move? Because that would grow tiresome.

I enjoyed being in charge, especially in the bedroom. But there was a limit to that control.

Perhaps I should keep her here and teach her how to live.

It'd be selfish on my part, knowing what her life would become after Blood Day. However, it might just make her final months here worth all the inevitable pain.

I could help give her positive memories to take to her grave.

Would that make it better or worse for her? I wasn't quite sure.

She entered the bath area behind me, but I caught her reflection in the windows framing the tub area. Her eyes widened as she took in the creamy stone floor and tiled walk-in shower. Then she admired the jeweled accents decorating the countertops and walls.

It certainly added an air of opulence to the room.

Every bathroom and bedroom had a collection of jewels, just in different colors.

The gemstones adorning my quarters were all rubies.

"A lot of the materials in the palace used to belong to wealthy humans," I told her. "I think they were going for a desert palace vibe from the days when sultans ruled this land, but they added some global opulence to it as well. However, the white stonework is all true to the region, keeping everything cool in the warmer months."

There was also a healthy bit of air-conditioning to keep everything cool, even in the open-aired courtyard in the middle of the property.

"They use solar energy to keep everything self-sustainable," I added, shrugging. "So it's like an ancient palace with upgraded technology."

And honestly not all that expensive to maintain as a result.

Just a lot of rooms to keep clean and ready for potential visitors.

"It's actually quite beautiful," I admitted as I switched off the water. It seemed to be high enough. "Maybe I'll give you a tour after our bath."

She might enjoy seeing some of the historical statues and the palm trees. The university grounds were barren, while the courtyards here flourished with life, thanks to the underground watering system.

Her gaze met mine as I faced her, then quickly dropped to the ground.

I caught her chin, pulling her focus back to me. "I don't expect formalities here, Lily. Now take off your clothes."

I was aware of the conflict of my statements—telling her not to bow in one sentence while demanding her obedience in the next—but I suspected she needed that to help ground her a bit.

Given how quickly she reacted, it seemed I was right.

She didn't hesitate in undressing, even going as far as to fold her garments on the marble counter. Then she moved them to the floor as though they were too dirty for the pristine surface.

I almost corrected her.

But she really wasn't wrong.

I'd have to find her new clothes to wear here.

Assuming I keep her.

The notion appealed to me more and more with each passing second. It'd be easy to negotiate. And I maintained the status to request it, too.

Although, it would potentially pique Silvano's interest.

And that would end very badly for Lily.

Decisions, decisions.

I returned to the bath to add the salts and check the temperature. It was warm without being too hot, at least to my sensitive touch.

"Can you test the heat and tell me if it's too much for you?" I asked, glancing at Lily.

Her brow furrowed as though she didn't understand the request, but she stepped forward to dip her hand in like I'd just done.

She didn't yank it back or hiss, telling me it was suitable.

"It's warm," she confirmed.

"Too warm or comfortably warm?" I pressed.

She blinked at me, then looked back down at the water. "It's... it's comforting."

"Good. Use the steps there to get in." I pointed to the stone stairs leading to the bath's entrance. I supposed it was more like a large pool than a tub, the benches inside providing enough space for five or six people.

There were jets, too. I'd turn those on once she was settled, as well as the purifier that would cycle the liquid and add fresh water periodically via the overhanging faucets on each side.

I grabbed some shampoo and body wash from the walk-in shower and set it on the side of the tub and noted Lily's stiff movements as she slowly moved to the stairs.

She swallowed, her pulse thrumming to life.

"Afraid of a little water?" I asked, amused.

But that amusement died when she started to shake.

Her spine straightened in the next instant, the brave part of her seeming to flicker into action. She climbed the steps to the top, her expression determined.

Then she moved to step down into the pool like she would on a normal stair and jolted as her foot touched the liquid. I jumped forward and caught her hips, holding her in place when she would have fallen.

She clearly had no idea what to do here.

"You've never been swimming or had a bath," I realized out loud. "Of course you haven't. Why would they indulge future slaves?"

I rolled my eyes at my own words, not at her, and gently helped her into the pool of water. She froze beneath my hands as her feet hit the bottom, obviously terrified of what would happen next.

Which completely defeated the purpose of the bath.

"Try not to move," I said as I released her. Her body locked in place when I stepped backward.

She didn't even appear to be breathing, her pulse beating wildly.

This wouldn't do at all.

I shucked off my pants, but left my boxers on, and moved up the steps to join her in the water.

She trembled as I grabbed her again, my body sliding in against hers. Which was precisely why I didn't lose my boxers. She was a temptation, and I needed the barrier between us.

Especially with how frightened she appeared to be.

I pulled her backward with me to one of the benches and sat down. She moved with me, not fighting me at all as I placed her in my lap. But her breathing remained shallow, her racing pulse a beacon that called to my prey drive.

"Baths are meant for relaxation, Lily," I said against her ear. "They're an indulgence meant to relax stiff muscles and clear your mind, but I should have realized it would have an opposite effect on you."

She remained silent, her heartbeat starting to slow. I gave her a few minutes, allowing her to acclimate while holding her back to my chest.

It wasn't the most comfortable position, so I shifted us longways on the bench with our legs stretched out, and relaxed against the wall behind me. When I pulled her back to my chest again, she stiffened.

"Are you worried I may drown you?" I wondered out loud as I pulled her long blonde hair over one shoulder. "You should be more concerned about my mouth being near your alluring neck."

I pressed a kiss to her throbbing pulse, the blood beneath singing to my instincts.

"I'm not going to hurt you, Lily," I promised against her throat. "Not today, anyway."

Or anytime soon, if I could help it.

"Why do you keep calling me that?" she asked, her voice lacking the fear I sensed in her scent.

"I've called you many things, darling. Be specific." I knew what she meant, but I wanted her to speak more.

"Lily," she replied. "Why do you call me Lily?"

"Because that's what you remind me of." I wrapped my

arm around her waist and used my opposite hand to grasp her chin to angle her head back toward me over her shoulder. "You have light hair, pale skin, long, stem-like legs, and you're beautifully delicate. Just like a lily flower."

She blinked long lashes at me. "A lily flower."

I nodded. "Lily for short."

"Like a name."

"Your name," I corrected. "It's sweeter than Prospect Four Hundred and Seven, Year One Hundred Seventeen, isn't it?" I understood the purpose of giving humans numbers instead of identities. But they were so fucking long.

"I like it," she whispered, her eyes holding mine. "Thank you."

I cupped her face and drew my thumb across her lips. "Just don't share it with anyone else. It'll be our little secret."

She swallowed. "Like your blood."

"Like my blood," I echoed in agreement. "We have a few secrets between us now."

Secrets that would inevitably lead to her death.

But that was a problem for another day.

Blood Day.

LILY

LILY.

My name is Lily.

Except names were only earned through immortality. His blood had done things to me, making me feel more alive than ever before. He'd healed me.

But I'm not immortal.

He'd said my name was a secret, just like his blood. So maybe he meant for this to be a name I used with him alone. Just like he didn't want me to call him Master Cedric here, merely Cedric.

What else did he want from me here?

We were in the water, his arm around me and his opposite hand on my chin. I wasn't sure how to react or what he wanted me to do. It was all so bizarre, so dreamlike, so *incredible.*

The water wasn't too hot. Nor was it cold. It felt good. Unlike any other water I'd experienced in a shower, where it was either scalding or frigid.

And this bath was huge.

At least three more people could join us in here, maybe more.

There were red jewels everywhere.

And a window that was frosted to disguise the outside.

"Can you go under the water for me?" Master Cedric asked, drawing my focus to him. He still held my chin, my face angled toward him over my shoulder, but my mind had wandered. "I'll hold you, if that's easier. But I need you to dampen your hair."

I blinked. I'd never been in water like this before, the depth going up to my belly button when I stood.

And now he wanted me to go under the surface? "Okay."

It wasn't like I could refuse him.

I tried to roll off him, but his arm clamped around my middle. Then he moved me through the water as though I weighed nothing—although, maybe I really was weightless because I certainly felt light in this pool—and cradled me against his chest with my legs tucked into a ball.

"Squeeze your nose between your thumb and finger. I'm going to dip you."

Frowning, I lifted my hand to do what he said, my lips parting to continue breathing.

"Close your eyes and hold your breath," he said, causing my heart to skip a beat.

This is dangerous.

He may drown me. End me. Kill me.

But why would he do that after healing me with his blood? Why would he do that after *naming* me?

Maybe because he wanted to play with his food? To give me a moment of hope before—

"Stop thinking and focus on how you feel," he said, his words cutting through my thoughts and forcing my attention to return to him.

Then he gradually dipped me backward just like he'd

warned he would do, except the water only covered my eyes, not my nose or mouth.

He lifted me until my ears were out of the water, my hair still mostly submerged. "How do you feel, Lily?"

"Light," I whispered, my voice nasally because of my pinched nose. "Nervous."

His arm left my shoulders, causing me to stiffen, but his hand cradled the back of my head, keeping me afloat. "I would teach you how to swim, but this isn't a proper pool. However, there's one outside, so perhaps I'll show you later."

How long am I staying here? I wondered. He'd spoken about a tour, and now he mentioned a pool outside. *What is happening?*

He ran his fingers through my hair, then guided me back to the bench and helped me sit between his legs. One of his feet remained on the marble bench while the other dropped off to touch the ground of the tub. I hugged my knees, my back to his front, but there was a clear space between us now.

I didn't feel as secure, the water a little too open.

But then his fingers returned to my hair, and a minty fragrance touched the air. *Shampoo,* I realized as he began running it through my strands. *He's washing my hair.*

No one had ever touched me like this, not even the groomers I met with every other week. When they washed my hair, it was with harsh water and plain soap. Which was quickly followed by sharp scissors for a trim.

But Master Cedric stroked me almost reverently.

Just like he had between my thighs, I thought, squeezing my legs together with the memory. It shot a tingle up my spine, stirring the hairs along my neck.

No one had ever touched me in that way either. So

masterful and knowing. Very unlike the tentative strokes of Six during our classes together.

And Six had certainly never made me fall apart like that. Not even close. I wasn't even sure I'd ever really come until today.

Maybe it had something to do with my heightened senses, but I suspected it had more to do with Master Cedric.

His fingers fisted in my hair, dragging me back into the water and forcing me to release my hold on my knees. I yelped at the abrupt movement, then plugged my nose before he yanked me all the way under. My eyes burned, reminding me to close them, and my heart raced in my chest.

What's he doing? Is he drowning me now?

I almost fought back, almost flailed my arms, but he lifted me to where my chin was above the water, allowing my lips to part and inhale air.

It was then that I realized my back was balancing on the thigh of his leg with the foot on the ground. He was keeping me safe while washing my hair.

Keeping me alive.

Healing me.

Grooming me.

I didn't understand any of this or why he felt the need to be kind.

But I refused to question him.

Lily, I marveled again. *He calls me Lily.*

A pretty name, so short and feminine. I liked the way it sounded on his lips, too.

He combed his fingers through my hair again, this time beneath the water, then righted me once more and pressed a kiss to my shoulder. "Good girl," he whispered, the words sending a shiver through my soul.

I'd pleased him.

I didn't really know how I'd done it, but I loved that I'd done something right.

More minty essence flooded my senses as a sponge appeared against my arm. Then he began to create suds that he worked into my skin. I watched from the corner of my eye, hypnotized by his movements.

They went all the way down to my fingertips, back up to my neck, and disappeared from view as he went under my hair to stroke my nape.

My back was next, the touch scattering goose bumps across my skin despite me being mostly submerged in the water.

I closed my eyes, enjoying the sensations.

Until the water flickered on beside us to release more liquid into the bath. I jolted, my gaze landing on the flowing faucet.

"It's going to help cycle some of the suds from the tub," he explained against my ear as he started on my opposite arm.

I swallowed, my nipples beading both from his touch and from his mouth being so close to my neck. He was awakening things inside me that I couldn't define. It was overwhelming and exciting and terrifying all at the same time.

His lips brushed my throat as the sponge left my arm for my abdomen. "Straighten your legs," he told me.

I did.

"Spread your thighs," he added in a low tone, his lips brushing my ear.

My heart skipped a beat, but I complied.

"Good girl," he said again, nuzzling my throat as the sponge ventured downward beneath the water.

He focused on my upper leg first, massaging my hip bone before skating along the top of my thigh.

Then he went inward, drawing the sponge upward to my intimate flesh.

I jolted as he touched my clit, pleasure zinging through my veins and forcing a gasp from my mouth.

"Sensitive?" he hummed against my ear.

"Yes," I admitted.

"Hmm." He did it again, then switched to my other leg, leaving behind an ache that felt oddly unfulfilled.

An ache that only increased as the sponge continued upward to my abdomen and breasts.

My eyes fell closed again, lost to his touch.

It felt like a dream.

A fantasy I hadn't realized I desired.

Another hint of the minty fragrance followed, the sponge coming alive with more suds that he worked into my skin. My nipples were so hard, his touch making my pulse race.

He circled my taut peak, then pinched one with his bare hand while he massaged soap into the other one. I leaned back against him, unable to hold myself upright. My chest felt tight, just like the area between my thighs. Like I was on the verge of another explosion, one that might just kill me.

But Master Cedric didn't appear to be in a hurry to coax it along.

Instead, he continued to torture me with that sponge, using soap as a distraction from what my body craved.

Until the bare hand on my breast ventured downward.

Pausing to trace a circle around my belly button.

Then all the way down to cup me between my legs.

I sighed his name, melting into him and his decadent touch.

His lips were on my neck, his tongue tracing my pulse, his voice a growl of sound I didn't fully understand. He could be saying he wanted to bite me, and I wasn't sure I'd react. Not with the way his touch felt against my intimate center.

He chuckled, the sound vibrating my back. His teeth skimmed my throat, whether from his grin or as a threat, I couldn't say.

I was too lost to him.

Too engrossed in the pleasure his touch evoked.

Too focused on his thumb circling the spot I wanted him to stroke most.

But his fingers entered me instead, the abrupt penetration causing me to flinch. Except he curled his touch upward, turning my flinch into a vibration of pleasure.

Pleasure he stoked by pressing his thumb to that place I desired.

"Cedric," I breathed, arching into his palm.

His other hand cupped my breast, the sponge having disappeared.

And his mouth sealed around my pulse.

Oh, Goddess...

The pinch of his incisors sent my heart into a chaotic rhythm that reverberated in my ears. A moment of panic sliced my consciousness, only to be swallowed by a volcano of heat that blanketed me in dark oblivion.

My orgasm wasn't gradual; it was immediate, ripping through me and spiraling me into a climax even more intense than before.

I lost the ability to see.

The ability to think.

The ability to breathe.

I became a liquid being thriving on ecstasy alone.

Throbbing. Pulsating. *Dying.*

But I couldn't even be mad or upset by it, not when it felt like this.

He was killing me and I didn't care.

Drinking me dry while wringing every ounce of rapture possible from my form.

The perfect death.

The perfect final moments.

The perfect *end*.

No more pain. No more wondering about my fate. No more fighting for an impossible future.

This was it, the darkness finally engulfing me for one final time.

I smiled. "Thank you." The words were a breath in my ears, but I wanted him to hear them, to know I appreciated him making this pleasurable.

"No, Lily. Thank you," he replied against my ear before returning to my neck and piercing me again.

Harsher this time.

More violent.

His hunger was a whiplash to my senses.

But the world had already begun to fade.

Into a perpetual darkness that I welcomed more readily than I probably should.

Until it all stopped.

The sensation.

The heat.

The pleasure.

And the sound of water draining followed.

Then I was wrapped up in a fluffy cloud of cotton and carried against a hard masculine chest to the bed I'd been in what felt like hours before.

My eyelids lifted, allowing me to meet Master Cedric's dark gaze. "Consider that your first lesson on relaxation," he said as he laid me in the bed. "I'm going to find something for you to eat. Just rest and recover."

He pressed a kiss to my forehead, leaving me confused and oddly cold.

He didn't kill me.

He bathed me. Pleasured me. Drank from me.

And now he'd just left me in his bed again.

Wrapped in a towel.

Gaping at the space he'd just occupied.

A lesson on relaxation.

Why?

To what purpose?

What lesson did he have in store for me next?

I shivered. Something about this game felt more dangerous than any I'd ever played. And for the first time in my life, I wasn't sure if I wanted to win.

Because passing these lessons might just end in the biggest failure of all.

A dangerous sense of optimism.

A desire to live.

A desire for *more*.

With Master Cedric.

A future that could never truly be mine, no matter how much I dreamed or fantasized about it.

"Try not to dream. Fantasies don't exist in your world anymore."

His words from the other day haunted me as I closed my eyes. This was all a game to him, a way for a predator to play with his food.

I pressed my fingers to my neck, feeling the already healing punctures in my skin. It grounded me in the present, chasing away my hope.

I might have enjoyed the sensations.

But that was all they were—pleasurable reactions to a predator's bite.

I sort of hoped the marks scarred my skin. I could use the constant reminder.

Because something about Master Cedric made me want to fall.

And if I gave in, I would truly drown.

It wouldn't be a quick death, but a slow and agonizing torment.

The kind of end that would chase me into the afterlife and haunt my soul.

Maybe that was his goal.

Maybe he wanted me to suffer.

I won't let that happen, I thought at him, my jaw clenching. *I refuse to be easy prey, Master Cedric. If this is a game, then you chose the wrong girl to play against. Because I will fight your mind games until my dying breath. I vow it.*

CEDRIC

My wrist buzzed as I entered the kitchen closest to my quarters. I glanced down to find a message from Silvano scrolling across my watch.

Of course.

It was like he'd sensed my temporary bout of pleasure and decided to kill it with a summons.

Rolling my eyes, I dismissed the message and started rummaging for food. I'd respond to his request in a day or two. Maybe three.

Not that it would help anything.

The tone of his reply implied he was running out of patience.

Blood Day isn't acceptable timing. Call me. —S

The words ran through my head a few times as I pulled some ingredients from the refrigerator. Silvano didn't typically issue edicts, but when he did, they were serious. Deadly so. If and when he demanded I accept the sovereign position, I wouldn't have a choice. Then I'd be forced to truly embrace this new world.

The university provided a healthy introduction to our reformed society.

And while I didn't enjoy it, I could ignore a lot of what was happening outside of the university walls.

Being a sovereign meant I could no longer fake the part. I would have to embrace it in full. To do otherwise would be dangerous. Those who refused to assimilate were either ousted or killed.

Those like Cam, the eldest of my kind who'd chosen to fight Lilith. He'd died.

As had all his followers.

And the new world had been born.

A world where Lily wilted more and more every day because humans were no longer allowed to bloom.

I stared down at the items on the counter, frowning at my options. They were my preferred snacks—cheese, deli meats, and a bit of jam. Far more decadent than the meal she'd eaten the other night.

Which meant these items would likely make her sick. Or worse, improve her tastes.

I couldn't torture her in that way. It wasn't fair or kind.

But I didn't have anything else in this kitchen to offer her.

So I pressed a button on the wall that I rarely ever used. A feminine voice came through a mere second later. "Yes, Sire?" The human slaves at this estate were always waiting for my requests, despite the fact that I barely called upon them.

"I need a human-appropriate meal," I told the girl. "Something with steamed vegetables, lean meat like chicken or turkey, a potato or some rice, and fruit as a dessert. Preferably strawberries, if we have them."

"Of course, Sire," she replied without missing a beat.

"Please have it delivered to my quarters," I added, putting the food away. "I'll meet you up there."

"Y-yes, Sire," she stammered, likely misinterpreting my need for her to deliver the food.

I didn't bother to correct her assumptions. She'd understand the purpose of the food as soon as she saw Lily and the puncture wounds in her slender neck.

I'd taken more blood than I should have from her, but her sweet scent had made me so damn hungry. I'd wanted to devour her in full while thrusting my cock deep inside her.

Alas, I'd held back.

I wanted her to beg me first, to truly want my touch before I gave it to her.

Of course, I'd done the opposite today.

However, I'd read the cues from her body and had reacted accordingly. She'd relaxed in response, her pleasure warming her very soul.

And enticing my predator that much more.

I hadn't been able to resist her throbbing pulse, so I'd bitten her. I wouldn't apologize for it, as I didn't want to lie. Just as I wouldn't promise not to do it again. Because I very much intended to sink my teeth into her naked flesh as many times as I could over the next few months.

Hence the need for her meal.

Lily would need her strength to survive my enhanced cravings. I might not have required much blood to thrive in this world, but that didn't mean I'd stop myself from indulging in her sweet taste.

She was a rarity. A treasure. A beacon of sunshine in a world of darkness. And I wanted her. So I would have her.

Did that make me a monster? To her, probably. But maybe she would understand my reasons in the end.

I'd try to help her.

I'd worship her, too.

If she desired more pleasure, I'd give it to her with my

tongue and body for as long as she required. I'd feed her. Bathe her. Give her the resources she needed to thrive.

For as long as this world allowed.

Maybe I would request that the university let me retain her for private lessons. It'd be a good way to keep her safe for her remaining months. Then I could fail her in the end, and her resulting death would be quick.

Perhaps they would even give me the honor of drinking her dry.

It'd be the kindest gift I could offer her in this world, even if she hated me for it. But I'd embrace that hatred over her pain.

That was the lesson I'd learned last night—that I could not stand to see her hurting.

It was why I'd reacted in a rash manner and brought her back here to heal her. I hadn't been able to handle her agony. I'd been irrationally inclined to save her myself.

Because she was mine.

I wanted her to leave this world on my terms, not those set by our society. Because the very thought of her torment killed me inside. She didn't deserve any of it. None of the humans really did.

But something about Lily made me even more displeased with the situation. I wanted to steal her away and hide with her for eternity.

A completely ridiculous fantasy, but one I idly entertained even as I ascended the stairs toward my quarters. I'd grabbed two bottles of water from the fridge, just in case the servant didn't bring any with the meal. It would take her maybe thirty minutes to prepare as well, and Lily likely needed a refreshment now.

My suspicions were confirmed as I entered my room to find her leaning against the headboard of my bed, still wrapped up in her towel. She appeared dazed, her skin pale, her eyes a light green rather than that blue-green shade.

I'd definitely taken too much blood from her. And she was suffering despite the healthy dose of my own essence last night. Perhaps because she'd used most of my supernatural energy to heal her other injuries.

I set the bottles down on the nightstand and joined her in the bed. She glanced at my bare abdomen and gray pajama bottoms and then up at my face.

I caught her cheek with my palm, then leaned in to kiss her softly on the lips. She shivered in response, her skin clammy beneath my hand.

Maybe I should rethink that apology, I thought.

She was too fragile for the amount of blood I'd taken from her, something I blamed society for more than myself. Had she been on a proper food regimen, she'd be fine right now. Alas, my little flower had been marked as a petite delicacy, one likely destined to be destroyed in a royal harem.

A lycan would break her immediately.

As would most vampires.

I would do my best not to follow suit, something I told her without words as I sliced my tongue along one of my canines and slipped it into her mouth.

She jolted in surprise, her eyes widening as I deepened our kiss by feeding her my blood.

My palm slid to her neck, my thumb drawing a line down her throat as a silent demand for her to swallow.

She obeyed.

I fed her more, giving her the essence that would help her heal and make her light-headed with immortality.

So forbidden.

So taboo.

So *dangerous*.

She wasn't the only one who could be punished for this. Although, I'd just say I'd wanted to keep my toy alive a little longer. Silvano would forgive it with a smirk, then either see how much her strengthened form could take before breaking or kill her outright.

Both outcomes irritated me, something I accidentally conveyed through my hand against Lily's throat. She flinched in response, and I immediately loosened my grasp.

"So delicate, my flower," I whispered, pressing my forehead to hers. "I don't mean to hurt you."

It was the closest I could come to an apology, the words meant more as an explanation than an excuse. She was just so inferior, which was part of my draw to her and also a deterrent.

I wanted her stronger. Fiercer. An equal. But that wasn't possible. To make her immortal would result in an immediate death sentence for her. And Silvano would be forced to punish me in that situation as well.

Vampires could no longer choose their progeny.

Over ninety percent of the human race had been exterminated, leaving us with a limited food source. Creating too many immortals would impact the blood rations.

Hence the need for the Immortal Cup. Only two humans were granted immortality every year, and their placement among the regions varied annually. Next year's picks would go to Clemente Clan and Jace Region.

My choice would be Jace in a heartbeat, and not just because of his vampire lineage. He ruled his territory with an air of fairness that most others in his position lacked.

Others like Alpha Walter of Clemente Clan.

Silvano, too.

The very concept of "fair" didn't apply to them. Let alone the notions of choice or equality or the desires of others within their regions. Rulers like Walter and Silvano only cared about their own needs.

But Silvano's penchants were a concern for another day.

I kissed Lily again, giving her more blood and sighing as I felt the power trickle through her being. By the time I pulled away, her eyes were brighter and widening with wonder.

"Vampire blood heals," I said, stating the obvious. "Which is why this is forbidden."

"A secret," she replied, echoing our conversation from last night.

"Yes." I brushed my lips across hers before leaning back to grab one of the waters. I twisted the cap and brought the bottle to her lips.

She swallowed greedily, confirming my predictions about her thirst. However, she winced a bit after a few gulps, so I pulled the bottle away and arched a brow.

"Cold," she said, wincing again.

She was probably used to room-temperature water, or worse.

I considered her for a moment, then took some liquid into my mouth to warm it before pressing my lips to hers. She jolted in surprise but opened her mouth and swallowed eagerly.

I repeated it, adding a little blood to it as well and giving her the nutrients she required to feel truly alive.

Her expression held so many questions when we finished the bottle, the blue in her multicolored irises glowing once more.

"You can speak freely," I said when she remained silent. "I won't punish you."

I set the empty bottle aside and settled next to her against the headboard. She still had her towel clutched around her like a shield. It'd be easy to demand that she remove it and converse with me naked, but that would lead to distractions. And I very much wanted her to voice some of the thoughts dancing behind those beautiful eyes.

"Why are you healing me?" she asked.

I shrugged. "Because I can. And because I want to." *Because you're mine.*

Well, not really.

But for now, I considered her mine.

"But why me? You... you hate me."

My eyes widened both at the statement and her bluntness. "I don't hate you, Lily. Quite the opposite, actually."

"But you keep failing me."

"That doesn't mean I dislike you," I replied, surprised by her correlation. "I told you why you're failing. That was the purpose of last night's lesson." It wasn't her fault. She just wasn't meant to be a Vigil.

She nibbled her lower lip. "I'm too small."

"Yes. However, that doesn't mean you're weak." I might call her delicate and fragile, but those words only applied to her physical form. "Strength isn't just about size."

"Are you saying there's another way to fight?"

"Not as a Vigil," I replied. "Not even really as a human." Which was perhaps what enthralled me about this situation. Lily possessed a fighting spirit, yet there was no outlet that allowed her to shine.

I wanted to give her an outlet with me. I just didn't know how to do it or what that desire even meant.

"Then what's the point?" she asked, a flicker of anger darkening her expression. "Why do any of this at all if there's nothing I can do? Why not just leave me alone and let me fail?"

I studied her. "Is that what you want?"

"Does it matter what I want?"

"In this world? No, not really." But in a past life, yes.

"Then why am I here?"

"Because I want you here," I answered unashamedly.

"But why?" Her cheeks were no longer pale but pink, her nostrils flaring in a clear sign of agitation.

It fascinated me to see so much emotion on her face, mostly because she normally controlled her features so flawlessly. But that façade was breaking now, and I wanted to force it to shatter.

"Do I need to have a reason to want you here, Lily?" I reached out to tuck one of her damp strands behind her ear. "Do I truly need to explain that decision to you?" I'd already told her I'd done it because I wanted to. What more did she need?

"No, I guess you don't," she replied, her voice holding a hint of bitterness that floored me.

"I don't," I agreed. But I would if she clarified her questions.

She grunted. "Right. Because you're the superior. If you want to play a game with me, I have no choice but to participate. And since you're the one making the rules, I'll inevitably fail like I always do."

My eyes widened at her little rant.

But she wasn't done.

"Which leads me back to wondering what the point is for all of this. Maybe you want to mess with me before you kill me. I just wish you'd tell me exactly what to do to expedite the results so I could get it over with." The last part came out in a grumble.

"My blood has made you quite bold," I mused.

Her jaw clenched. "You healed me just to fuck with

me. This is all probably some test you've designed for me to fail, too."

"I am not *fucking* with you," I bit back, not at all pleased by her accusation. Mostly because it made me wonder whether or not she was right. It'd been so long since I'd entertained a female that I really couldn't define my intentions anymore. Not in this world.

"Yes, you are!" she screamed, shocking the hell out of me.

Which, of course, was the exact moment that two other things happened at once.

Someone knocked on the door—likely the servant with her food.

And my wrist started buzzing with an incoming call from Silvano. Apparently, he wasn't waiting for my reply.

Fuck.

LILY

"GO ANSWER THE DOOR," MASTER CEDRIC DEMANDED. "I need to take this call. If you value your life, you'll remain silent."

Some irrational part of me wanted to scream just to scream. He'd told me to speak freely, then responded to my questions with half-answers.

"Why am I here?"

"Because I want you here."

What the Goddess did that even mean?!

Then he'd said this wasn't a game when clearly—

"Prince Silvano," he greeted, cutting off my thoughts with a shot of ice down my spine. A screen appeared in front of him to reveal a male with long white hair, dark eyes, and a perfectly square jaw.

"Cedric. I told you to call me." The slight accent curling around his tone made me shiver. As did the recognition working its way through my mind.

Royal vampire.

A royal vampire who just called Master Cedric.

Master Cedric, who I just yelled at.

Me. I yelled. No, I did more than that. I screamed at him.

Oh, Goddess, I'm—

"Yes, my apologies, My Prince. I saw your message as I was enjoying my breakfast and became distracted," Master Cedric replied, disappearing from the bedroom through a set of sliding doors that led to the balcony outside. He closed the glass slats behind him, cutting me off from the conversation.

A conversation with a royal vampire.

Because Master Cedric is important.

High-ranking.

And I just—

Another knock sounded, the rapping noise reminding me of a drum counting down the seconds to my inevitable death.

"Go answer the door," Master Cedric had demanded.

I stole a sharp breath, trying to calm my beating heart. But I'd just done the unthinkable. I'd verbally sparred with a superior, and a high-ranking one at that. A future sovereign.

Prince Silvano's progeny.

That practically made Master Cedric royalty himself, or very well near it. Which explained his stay here at—

Another knock interrupted my thoughts, making me scurry off the bed. I needed to obey Master Cedric, to prove I could... I could... *Oh, I don't even know anymore.*

This game between us had rules I didn't understand.

He was unlike any of my prior Masters, his behavior something I'd always feared from his kind, as I'd seen what happened to humans who caught the eye of superior beings.

Except he'd been mostly kind.

Feeding me. Healing me. Giving me water.

But what is waiting for me behind this door? I wondered as I approached it. I still had my towel wrapped around me, which was better than nothing. For some reason I felt the need to wear the fabric as armor, which was ridiculous, considering how often I was forced to walk around without clothes.

Regardless, I held the knot at my chest as I used my opposite hand to open the door.

A petite human female stood outside holding a tray, her gaze averted. "I'm sorry for knocking more than once, Sire. Mistress Adrienne t-told me to kn-knock again," she stammered, her skin a sheet of white against her darker features.

"Master Cedric is in the other room," I whispered, trying to keep my voice as low as possible. He'd told me not to speak. But maybe he'd just meant as he answered the phone. Or maybe he'd meant now.

I didn't know.

I didn't really know anything at all.

The human didn't acknowledge me, her gaze still on the ground. "Master Cedric asked for me to deliver this."

I assumed *this* was the tray in her hands. "Oh." I stepped backward into the room to search for an appropriate place to set it down, but the female moved in after me and went straight toward the bedroom. "He just took a call out on the balcony," I warned her. "With Prince Silvano."

She froze, then turned abruptly. Her hands were shaking as she set the tray down on a table near the corner of the room. It seemed like an odd choice, given the larger table near the two couches in the center.

I nearly asked, but she fell to her knees onto the marble floor beside the table, taking a submissive pose without a word. Then she unbuttoned the top of her shirt to make her neck more accessible.

And bent her head next before going perfectly still.

Did Master Cedric intend to feed from her after already biting me today? Would he give her blood afterward?

Was this another lesson of some kind?

He'd told me to answer the door and not speak.

Okay, so what now? Did I bow like her? Kneel and await my fate?

A fate that couldn't be good, considering I'd just screamed at him.

What was I thinking? How could I be so free with my emotions?

Maybe it was his blood. It left me feeling alive. Invincible. *Strong.* And I hated how grateful that made me, how indebted to him I felt for giving me such an amazing sensation.

Oh, and the pleasure. Dear Goddess, he'd awakened a warmth in me that I wanted to experience again and again. Which terrified me, given that it was *him* evoking those feelings.

As though I needed another reason to be drawn to him.

He was handsome. Powerful. Intimidating. Strong. And now I had to add *giving* to the list. *Considerate.* A man possessing a rapturous touch.

I nearly groaned, my thighs tingling with awareness all over again.

I wanted him.

Yet I disliked him.

Well, no. I *feared* him. Except I also didn't.

And I'd screamed at him. Yeah, back to that transgression again.

I'd been so focused on fighting him, on looking for a way to play this game, that I'd grown frustrated by his responses.

What's he going to do to me now?

Maybe I should kneel with the other girl. At least that would give me a somewhat contrite appearance.

Swallowing, I decided to do just that.

I dropped the towel and went to the floor near the table. Master Cedric had wanted me naked and kneeling during our first private lesson. Maybe if I did this now, he'd indulge me in a punishment rather than kill me outright.

Although, I wasn't sure the former would be much better.

Goddess, I'm a mess. I'd lost my head completely, forgotten all my training, and verbally assaulted a superior. Surely that hadn't been his desire when he'd told me to speak freely.

My knees protested a bit against the marble floor. Kneeling on the plush carpet of the bedroom or even the rug in the decorative seating area would have been preferable. But I assumed this other human knew Master Cedric's preferences.

I kept my head down and started counting.

When I reached a thousand, I started over.

Once I hit the number again, I went back to one.

It kept me calm and helped me control my breathing.

I was on my seventh round of the nine hundreds when Master Cedric finally returned. His steps were silent, but I felt his presence like a whip against my senses.

Anger.

Irritation.

Hunger.

I experienced each emotion as though they were my own. But they weren't mine. They were *his*. Was he projecting? Had imbibing his blood done something to connect us? Was I picking up on his emotions because of my enhanced state of being?

"Leave us," he said, his voice deep and commanding. "*Now.*"

Who is he talking—

The other female hopped up to her feet and scurried from the room, leaving me behind on my knees before I could finish processing my thought.

Am I supposed to follow? Was it a test to see who ran first? What does he want me to do? Is this—

"Stand up, Lily." His voice maintained that lethal edge to it, his fury prickling my neck and showering goose bumps down my arms.

My throat constricted, making it difficult to swallow or breathe.

Stand up, I coached myself. *Stand up right now.*

A jolt spasmed along my thighs as I forced myself to move, my knees aching from the sudden blood flow through my limbs. But the sting abated almost instantly.

I didn't meet Master Cedric's stare. Instead, I kept my head bowed and waited for further instruction.

He snorted, the sound harsh and abrupt and underscored with irritation. "Weren't you just accusing me of *fucking* with you?"

I winced. Not only had I screamed at him, but I'd cursed, too. Humans weren't supposed to use that kind of language around their superiors. It was classified as insulting behavior. "I'm sorry, Master Cedric. I forgot my place. I'll accept whatever punishment you wish to deliver."

"I don't have time to punish you, let alone correct you," he retorted. "That tray is full of food for you. Eat it. I need to make a few more calls."

He didn't wait for a response or my agreement, his presence leaving mine in a wave of irritation as he returned to the balcony.

I nibbled my bottom lip. *The tray is for me?*

Master Cedric had said something about food earlier, but he'd returned with water and I'd forgotten all about my stomach. I also wasn't nearly as hungry as I usually would be at this time of the night. Because of his supernatural blood or my raging nerves, I wasn't sure.

However, I crept toward the tray anyway to investigate the contents.

A cup of rice. Grilled meat. Green vegetables. And a strange red fruit.

Strawberries, I thought, recalling a visual of this berry from long ago. I'd never actually had one before.

I picked up that item first and took a bite. Sweetness touched my tongue, making me groan at the delectable flavor.

It was almost too much, the sugar going straight to my head. But I devoured it anyway and enjoyed a second one before switching to the vegetables.

The servings reminded me of the bag Master Cedric had given me the other night. I usually received a quarter of this amount of food, but the more I ate, the hungrier I became.

I was picking up my final strawberry—something I'd saved for last on the tray—when Master Cedric returned. He paused on the threshold of the room, watching as I brought the fruit to my mouth.

Part of me wondered if I should stop.

The other part of me couldn't because I really wanted that piece of fruit.

He said nothing as I bit into it and swallowed, his dark eyes going to my throat before trailing a hot path down my still-naked form.

I'd eaten while standing beside the tray, as I hadn't known where to sit. I also hadn't really considered sitting down. The meat and vegetables had already been cut into bite-size pieces, making it easy to spear them with the fork. I'd been too consumed with the strawberries to focus on much else. They were my reward for finishing the other items on the tray.

Master Cedric started toward me as I popped the rest of the strawberry into my mouth, his palm wrapping around my throat as I started chewing.

"You're supposed to remove the stem part," he said, his thumb massaging the side of my throat. "It's not bad for you, but it can alter the flavor."

As the taste hadn't bothered me with the others, I swallowed.

His gaze narrowed, then he released me and turned toward his bedroom once more. "Follow me. You need clothes."

Irritation and hunger continued to roll off of him, the emotions an intoxicating cloud that swirled around me as I trailed behind him.

He pressed a button on the wall. "I need clothes for a human. She's five-foot-four and petite."

"Of course, Sire," a male voice responded. "Would you like them in your quarters?"

"Yes. And I don't need blood, so don't come in here and kneel. I've already been fed."

"Of course, Sire," the voice repeated. "Anything else?"

"Shoes for the human, too." He glanced at my feet and accurately guessed my size. "Nothing else."

The male reiterated the same phrase, then the room fell silent.

Master Cedric faced me, his expression giving nothing away. "You'll tell no one about your experiences here. You'll forget the name I provided for you. And if anyone asks about your miraculous recovery, you'll tell them your injuries weren't severe or that you faked them. Understood?"

My throat felt tight again, my mouth dry, which made my voice a bit raspy as I replied, "Yes, Master Cedric."

"Good. Answer the door when they knock. Get dressed. I'll return you to the university in an hour." With that, he left again for the balcony. The sliding glass doors seemed to slam behind him with a finality that said whatever this had been was done.

We were done.

And I was left gaping after him, never having understood the game at all.

He hadn't even given me a chance to properly play.

Which is what I wanted, right?

But if that was the case, why did I feel so cold and empty?

I shivered, suddenly feeling more naked than seconds ago.

I slid into the bed, wrapping myself in the sheets and wishing I could turn back time to when I'd woken up with his body pressed against mine.

I'd been warm.

Alive.

Exhilarated.

Now I just felt dead inside. *Alone.*

He'd taken away my name. My new identity. My forbidden sense of hope.

"You'll forget the name I provided for you."

Lily.

I hadn't truly realized what that had meant to me until he'd taken it away and reduced me to nothing but a number again.

Prospect Four Hundred and Seven.

Master Cedric had given me a dose of something I

didn't quite understand, then reversed it in the next breath. It left me wondering what else he could have shown me.

It made me want to fix this.

To fight for my new name.

Because I didn't want to be Prospect Four Hundred and Seven.

I wanted to be Lily.

His Lily.

The realization struck me deep in the chest, squeezing my heart and stealing the air from my lungs.

So how do I fix this?

LILY

Master Cedric didn't return until I was dressed and ready to go. He glanced over my white dress, stockings, and flat shoes. The curl of his lip didn't seem to be a favorable reaction, not with the way he grunted afterward.

But he didn't comment.

All he did was nod his head in a *follow me* gesture before leading me through the immaculate palace. I was momentarily awestruck by the opulence around me. It reminded me of his quarters, only the glittering gems shifted colors along the white-and-cream textured walls.

He took me through a courtyard with a fountain surrounded by palm trees. My fingers itched with the desire to touch one of the spiny leaves, but he was moving too fast for me to pause.

This place was nothing like the university grounds.

Spindles of gold were etched into the arches of the various entryways outside, with glimmers of it glinting off the moonlight on the tops of the cone-shaped towers in the corners of the compound. So much grandeur and beauty.

This is his life.

The life of a high-ranking vampire.

An old vampire.

One with ties to royal blood.

I swallowed, my gaze sliding to the back of his head. He moved with the grace of a predator, silent and sleek and lethal. But there was an edge to his steps that hadn't been there before. His spine was rigid, his hands loose at his sides. Almost as though he were ready to engage in battle.

My heart skipped a beat as I wondered if I was the intended target.

But he merely led me into another section of the palace, down a large grand hall that stretched three stories high, and out the massive front doors.

A car sat idling at the bottom of the stone steps with a human standing beside it, head bowed.

Master Cedric took something from the male's hands. "You're dismissed."

The human didn't reply, instead choosing to walk steadily away from the parked car. But he didn't head up the main stairs. He started off down a sidewalk that seemed to lead to another building.

"In," Master Cedric demanded, returning my attention to where he stood with the car door open.

I slid into the bucket seat without a word, doing my best to obey his every command. His mood suggested that doing otherwise would end badly.

He leaned in over me, dragging a buckle across my lap and clicking it into place.

The door slammed in the next second, his body moving too fast for me to comprehend.

And he was in the seat beside me a blink later.

My heart hammered against my ribs, his vampiric speed leaving me winded as though I'd been the one who'd moved that quickly.

He started the car in the next instant, his foot hitting the pedal and shooting us forward.

I swallowed my scream, my training kicking in and forcing me to take hold of my emotions. But I couldn't stop my thundering pulse or my harsh intake of breath.

"Relax," Master Cedric muttered. "I'm not going to hurt you, Prospect."

Prospect. Not Lily.

"But if you breathe a word of anything we've shared to anyone else, you will die." His tone resembled a blade, sharp and lethal and intimidating. "Keep our secrets safe and you'll prolong your survival."

I'd already agreed to do so, but I whispered, "Yes, Master Cedric," again just to make sure he knew I'd heard both of his warnings.

He said nothing else as he navigated the pitch-black roads, the moon and his car's headlights the only illumination around us.

Until we reached the Blood University gates.

Then light flooded the surrounding walls, making it almost resemble daylight.

A pair of Vigils gave Master Cedric access without comment, allowing him to drive inside and park. I vaguely remembered him phasing us here after class. *Was that just last night?* It felt like at least a week ago.

He was out of the car almost as fast as he'd entered it, reaching my side and pulling open the door before I could even start to process the time change.

His fingertips brushed my hip as he found the buckle, then he reared back as though I'd burned him.

I really messed this up, I thought, swallowing as I moved to exit the car. I should have tried to talk to him on the way back, but I hadn't been able to think much beyond controlling my reactions to him. And he was radiating so much furious energy that I felt choked by his presence.

I half expected him to slam the door, get back in the car, and leave me standing here. But he instead went to the trunk and retrieved a familiar bag—the one I used for my books and supplies.

He pulled it over his shoulder rather than handing it to me, shut the trunk, and started walking with another one of those nods.

I almost had to run to keep up with him as he stomped across the bare courtyard outside—the sand was much less beautiful than the palm trees and fountains we'd walked through not even thirty minutes ago—toward the residential area of campus.

I kept my head down in the way I'd been taught, following him without question.

No one was outside, suggesting we'd returned during one of the free-day studying hours. We usually had a mandated exercise activity upon waking, then breakfast, then study hours, until eventually being allowed sixty minutes to wander the grounds before dinner.

I recently started using that free hour to practice my fighting routines outside where I had more room to move.

Almost everyone kept to themselves, as frequent fraternization wasn't recommended. There were some students who studied together, but most preferred to work on projects alone. At the end of it all, we were competing for the same positions. It didn't benefit us individually to help others.

Although, I sometimes sat with Six and assisted him with certain topics. His doing well in a course tended to suit both of us since we were often partnered.

The silence inside the residential hall confirmed that we'd returned during a study period. All the doors were closed, including that of the resident lycan who supervised this wing.

"Just returning a prospect," Master Cedric said suddenly.

My brow furrowed. *What?*

"No. I have it handled," he added as the resident lycan's door opened.

Master Telisca appeared in a pair of jeans and a tank top, her expression curious as she looked us over.

"Interesting choice," she mused, making me realize that Master Cedric had been talking to her through the door.

His enhanced senses must have allowed him to hear her, just as her lycan ears would have alerted her to our presence. She had probably been able to smell us, too.

"You say that as though your opinion matters to me," Master Cedric replied, walking right by the tall, redheaded lycan and heading in the direction of my room. "As I said, I have this handled."

"Yeah, yeah," she huffed, her hazel eyes flickering with her wolf before she stepped back into her room.

I skipped forward to catch up to Master Cedric, my heart in my throat. I didn't want to risk Master Telisca reappearing and grabbing me, something I'd seen her do before.

Those humans always disappeared. For good.

And new ones appeared to replace them.

I'd never understood how any of that worked, whether they came from somewhere within the university or outside of it.

Many of us were shifted around often between the various residences.

However, I'd been in this one for the last four or five years. Maybe even six. I'd lost count.

Master Cedric didn't ask me for a room number or what floor I lived on. He ascended two sets of stairs without a word and led me straight to my single bedroom.

He tried the handle.

"Study hours," I whispered. "The doors—"

He flipped open a keypad beside my door, silencing me as he entered a code too fast for me to see. A hissing sound followed, then the lock on my door unlatched, allowing him to push through the threshold.

Because of course he knew about the auto-lock process.

He was a Master at the university.

Why did that suddenly feel like a revelation or a remembrance? How had I so easily forgotten what this vampire represented?

He set my bag on the room's lone chair, right in front of my desk. I followed him inside and took in my small bed, single dresser, and the porthole window allowing some moonlight into my room.

It all seemed so dull in comparison to his lavish quarters.

He'd changed out of his pajamas before we'd left, which only seemed to make him stand out more now as he stood in the center of my room in his all-black suit. He clashed considerably with the white stone floor and the cream-colored walls.

His dark eyes found mine, sending a chill down my spine. I immediately lowered my gaze. But he stepped forward and caught my chin, forcing me to meet his stare.

His irises resembled a storm, the obsidian rings vibrating with thunderous emotion. An apology sat heavily on my tongue. As did a plea for forgiveness.

Words whispered through my mind as well. Forbidden ones that begged him to take me back to his palace. *Just one more night. Let me escape this existence for a little bit longer. Please.*

But my voice failed me.

I couldn't speak.

His touch shifted to my cheek, his gaze falling to my mouth as though he was waiting for whatever I might say.

Nothing came. No air. No appropriate words. No cohesive sentence. No confession or apology or whatever he needed to hear. I just stood before him like a worthless pet, utterly lost to my emotions and the confusion of the last twenty-four hours.

"Already wilting," he murmured, his thumb tracing the hollow beneath my eye. "It's a cruel world, little flower. I wish you were born in a different time."

He pressed his lips to mine before I could even fathom a reply. It wasn't like the other kisses we'd shared. This one seemed final somehow, almost cold.

At least until his tongue slid into my mouth.

His palm moved to the back of my neck, his grip harsh as he commanded me with his touch. I melted into him, lost to the sensation of his presence.

He was so strong, so domineering, it was impossible to think of anything else while he held me in his arms.

Which was why I swallowed automatically, completely under his thrall.

Ambrosia, some part of me registered. *He's giving me his blood again.*

Not copious amounts like he had from his wrist, but just a little from his tongue. Enough to renew my spirits and stroke my senses back to life. I was still high on his essence from before; this just emboldened the sensations and made them that much deeper.

Was he trying to remind me of our secret? Or was he testing my resolve to remain quiet?

I wasn't sure.

And my mind refused to process any potential responses to the questions.

All I wanted was him, his mouth, his taste, his *tongue*.

But he pulled away, breaking our kiss, and slid his lips along my jaw to my neck.

His fangs pierced my throat in the next instant, making my legs buckle from the unexpected intrusion. A muscular band—*his arm*—wrapped around my back, holding me upright as his opposite hand remained around my nape.

I succumbed to him, allowing him to drink, dazed from the flavor of his blood and the pleasure of his bite.

My veins burned.

My stomach clenched.

And my thighs rubbed together to create necessary friction.

I barely recognized myself, this wanton version of me so different from the one who'd wanted to be a Vigil. She still existed deep down. Maybe. I'd search for her later.

Master Cedric's leg slid between mine, his muscular thigh pressing into my heated center and giving me the pressure I needed.

I moaned.

He growled.

Then the mattress of my bed met my back, startling me back into reality.

Master Cedric still had one leg between mine with his knee planted on the bed, but his arm was no longer around my back. His hands were on my shoulders instead, pinning me beneath him as he pressed his mouth to my ear.

"Careful," he whispered. "Prospects don't react."

His words sent a chill down my spine.

He'd told me to react earlier, to scream for him, to allow him to hear my pleasure.

And now he was telling me not to react.

He was reminding me of my place, taking away the brief glimpse of freedom he'd allowed from the university walls.

A cruel trick. A harsh punishment.

"Master Cedric," I breathed, wanting to apologize, to go back to being his Lily.

But his palm covered my mouth. "Silence, Prospect." The ice in his tone drilled a hole right through my spirit, leaving me hollow and frozen beneath him.

He bit me again, cascading a wave of heat over my form that threatened to thaw me from my frigid state. I clamped down on my lower lip to hold back my scream, the sound one of agony mingled with pleasure.

Tears filled my eyes.

My world spiraling out of control in a blink.

I wanted to lift my hips against his.

I wanted to shove him off of me.

I wanted to scream an apology against his mouth.

I wanted to dig my nails into his shoulders to hold on for dear life and beg him to take me back to his palace.

I wanted to disappear and forget him entirely.

All at once, every single desire mixed inside me, threatening to overwhelm my control. Years of training kicked in, attempting to push it all down, to keep me from reacting. But I couldn't stop the lone tear from escaping my eye.

Master Cedric's thumb swiped it away, his palm still covering my mouth. Then his thigh pressed into my core, causing electricity to hum through my being and zap my heart into overdrive.

It was too much sensation.

Too much *emotion*.

I was going to explode. Scream. *Shatter*.

His lips captured mine as I tumbled into oblivion, my body vibrating from the onslaught of fire and ice mating inside my veins.

It stirred chaos inside me. Burning. Shivering. Screeching for release.

Oh…

I cried out, but he caught the sound with his tongue, his blood filling my mouth and forcing me to swallow.

I gagged, coughed, sputtered, but he demanded that I take it, accept it, *embrace* it.

All while his eyes held mine, conveying some hidden message I couldn't understand.

By the time he finished, my soul felt ripped to shreds. I couldn't breathe or process what'd just happened.

He glared down at me in disgust, his expression one I would never forget.

Fury.

Hatred.

Sadness.

I trembled, not liking this turn of events at all.

He'd just ruined every kiss, every moment, every *memory*, we'd created.

Dead. Gone. *Destroyed.*

Just like my name. Just like my hope.

He pressed his forehead to mine, his breath feathering over my lips. "Consider this our final lesson," he whispered, his words oddly sounding like a goodbye. Just like the way our kiss had started. A finality lurked between us. One I couldn't quite define.

Because he no longer wished to play this game?

Because he no longer wanted to torture me?

Because he was about to kill me?

All of the notions were possible outcomes.

His lips brushed mine a final time, then he stood, his

shoulders rigid, his gaze giving nothing away. He glanced once at my neck, and in the next instant, he was gone.

The door to my room slammed, sending a jolt down my spine.

My chance for voicing an apology was gone.

And now I had no idea what tomorrow would bring.

Another test? Another failure? More of his blood?

I blinked, my heart still racing in my chest.

Another chill swept over me, a sense of dread unfurling inside my heart.

Somehow, this entire exchange felt like my biggest failure to date, like I'd done something incredibly wrong. Like I'd ruined my chance at experiencing something *more*.

It'd been there for a second. A brief moment in time.

Leaving me with nothing.

Just a hollow soul.

A rapidly beating heart.

And the sense that tomorrow would become one of the worst days of my life. Perhaps even my last.

LILY

I woke up to the scent of mint kissing my senses.

My lips tingled as though I could taste it.

And I did.

In my mouth.

Down my throat.

Into my very being.

Except it wasn't real.

As I stirred, I found myself staring at a white wall, not opulent furnishings and gemstones.

Just my cement prison. My room. My real life.

Did I dream it all? I wondered, sitting up to touch my neck. Smooth skin met my fingertips, causing me to frown.

Then I remembered Master Cedric's blood and the healing properties that came with it.

My bag was on the chair, right where he'd left it.

Or had I put it there?

A glance at the clock told it was time to rise for the evening. A new day of classes would begin soon. I needed to shower, then have breakfast.

I rolled off my bed, noting that I still wore my clothes from yesterday. Which confirmed everything had been real, that Master Cedric had called that bite his final lesson.

He couldn't have made his dismissal any clearer.

But part of me didn't want to accept that. Part of me wanted to fight his decision. To prove him wrong. To make him reconsider.

My jaw clenched. Maybe that was exactly what I needed to do. What did I have to lose? He'd already taken away my taste of another life, leaving me with nothing once more.

Of course, he could kill me.

However, that risk applied to all the monsters at this school.

So what did I really have to lose?

I wanted another chance to play his game—whatever it meant—and try to win. It was probably rigged for me to fail, but at least I'd feel alive again. Even if for only a few brief moments, it would be worth it to escape this repetitive existence.

He'd shown me another side of the world, gifted me with pleasure and excitement, and I craved more. Another bite. Intense sensation. *Rapture.*

I would tell him what I wanted after class tonight by kneeling for him. And if he denied me, I'd do it again. And again. And again.

Yes, that's exactly what I'll do, I thought as I walked over to my dresser to pull out a new outfit. However, a glint of something in my closet caught my attention, pulling me away from the drawer and toward the slightly ajar door.

Frowning, I pulled it open the rest of the way and found several cases of water stacked all the way up to the ceiling.

I blinked. There had to be hundreds of bottles in here.

Was this a new way to deliver our rations? To test our ability to not overindulge in resources?

The few dress garments I owned were pushed to the side, and my shoes were now on the top shelf. Everything else was water. At least six months' worth, by the looks of it, maybe more.

I took one from the plastic and twisted the cap to take a sip. This might be a test, too. Maybe it was poisoned, but I was too parched to deny the bottles before me. I'd skipped dinner last night, having fallen asleep beneath a wave of self-pity.

The water tasted normal. It was lukewarm, so not nearly as refreshing as the liquid Master Cedric had provided, but it satisfied my thirst. I finished half of it, then set it back in the case and waited to see if I felt any different.

I didn't notice anything other than feeling slightly more hydrated than before.

All right. I shut the door and went to find clothes from my dresser, then took them with me to the communal bathrooms to shower. I waited for one of the others to mention the new water bottle distribution, but no one said a word.

That wasn't abnormal—most of us didn't talk.

But sometimes we would whisper about changes, and this seemed significant enough to discuss.

Or maybe that was just me overthinking it.

I prepared for the day, took another sip of the water in case I wouldn't receive any other bottles today, and headed to breakfast.

Where I was given a larger ration than my usual.

Instead of one scoop of eggs, they gave me three. Just as I received a full piece of toast, not half of one. And they gave me an orange instead of a celery stick.

As well as another bottle of water.

I didn't say anything, my face carefully neutral as I accepted my plate.

But inside I was alive with questions.

Why had they changed my food regimen?

I cautiously ate all of it, my gaze darting around to others to see if anyone else was eating more than usual. Except it was hard to judge because I rarely paid attention to the food portions of others.

No one appeared surprised, though. They were likely masking their emotions just like me, making it impossible to know if any of them were experiencing these abnormalities.

I remained vigilant throughout my first class, searching for signs of anything out of the ordinary. But everyone acted the same as always.

Today's assignment revolved around maid services, specifically in the bedroom. We were timed on how fast we could make a bed in the particular ways Master Clarissa had shown us the other day.

I found my steps moving quicker than usual, my hands more efficient, and my confidence higher.

Perhaps because of Master Cedric's blood still flowing through my system. Everything was still heightened. Or maybe it was from the increase in food.

Regardless, Master Clarissa gave me high marks and stated the others in the class needed to be more efficient —*like me*.

I didn't react to her praise. Instead, I focused on keeping my expression vacant as she began a new tutorial in bedroom-cleaning etiquette—how to handle soiled linens. She demonstrated on blood-soaked sheets that were likely fresh from a kill.

My stomach churned at the sight of it, my mind

wandering to Master Cedric's bite.

He hadn't been cruel so much as sensual.

But I wasn't naïve enough to consider that to be a normal experience.

Actually, nothing about Master Cedric could be described as *normal*. He was an enigma that I didn't understand.

An enigma that I intended to face off against tonight.

That was the thought that followed me throughout my evening, lurking in the back of my mind through each lecture and activity.

My blood practically thrummed with nervous excitement when the time for his class neared.

Except he wasn't the vampire waiting for us in the classroom.

A dark-haired male with turquoise eyes stood in his place, his black jeans and matching T-shirt stretched tight across a body made of solid muscle.

Lycan, my mind guessed immediately as I dropped my gaze to the ground.

He introduced himself as Master Khalid and promptly reorganized the pairings in our class. He placed me with a male closer to my size—my former female partner was notably missing—and put the two massive men together again.

Then he went into a lesson without any comment as to Master Cedric's absence.

Not that I expected an explanation. I was a human, not an equal. But it took every ounce of willpower not to ask.

Maybe this is temporary, I thought. *Maybe he'll be back tomorrow.*

Except he wasn't back in the next class.

Or the one after that.

Or the one after that, either.

Four weeks passed with no sign of Master Cedric. It seemed as though Master Khalid had officially taken over, which I should have been thankful for because I was finally passing some of the tests in this course.

But I found myself longing for Master Cedric. He haunted my dreams—dreams I knew I shouldn't have of him.

Those dreams worsened as his blood fully left my system, returning my senses back to normal. It was as though I'd lost the final piece of him, leaving me with just fantasies.

Fantasies that flourished wildly in my mind while I slept.

The increased food rations continued as well with a small lunch being added to my daily agenda. I felt rejuvenated and stronger with each passing day, almost similar to how Master Cedric's blood had made me feel.

Only it wasn't the same.

Some twisted part of me missed him.

Which was why I found it hard to say his name now as my advisor asked me for an update on my courses.

I was seated on my bed, staring at her image against my wall. She appeared every few weeks to discuss my schedule, and originally, I'd intended to use our next session to discuss Master Cedric's class. Now I just wanted to ask her where he'd gone and if I could enroll in one of his other courses.

However, my training kicked in as I provided her with an update on my classes and how I felt they were going. I even told her that I believed my fighting skills were finally improving.

"Yes, I see that here in Master Khalid's notes," she replied, her gaze flicking away from me as she scrolled through her tablet. "It seems Master Cedric had his doubts, but his advice to increase your food rations has helped. Of course, your weight is fluctuating, too. So we'll have to decide if that's the appropriate route for you."

Master Cedric advised you to increase my food rations? I nearly asked, my mind reeling from that reveal.

Although, part of me had already wondered if he'd been the reason behind my new food schedule.

Just as I wondered if he'd been the one to stock my closet full of water.

Because no one had mentioned any of it and the cafeteria matrons continued to give me the same amount of bottles every day. I almost asked my advisor, but some part of me whispered a warning to remain silent.

It was the same part of me that remembered his warning to keep our secrets between us.

If I mentioned the water, they might take it from me.

Or maybe that was part of the test.

Regardless, I chose not to say anything.

It felt a bit like a rebellion, as though I were breaking an unspoken rule to reveal everything to my advisor at all times.

I rather liked keeping the knowledge to myself and not sharing it with her.

"However, he also noted your sexual skills are quite lacking, so your weight may not be an issue after all," she continued, cutting through my thoughts and slapping me across the face with her words.

He noted what?

"He actually strongly recommended your routine be shifted to servitude courses rather than sexual arts, stating that he didn't feel you'd be adequate enough for a harem. And obviously, he wasn't impressed with your fighting skills." She uttered the words plainly and without emotion, like she wasn't punching me with each syllable.

All I kept hearing was, *Master Cedric noted your sexual skills are quite lacking.*

In what way?

Because I'd moaned while he'd fed me that last time? Because I hadn't moaned initially? *What did he want from me?!*

"It's disappointing, as Master Peyton gave you high marks in oral sex. But Master Clarissa has also confirmed your aptitude for the service industry."

My advisor finally looked at me again.

"So we have a few choices on courses for the next round. Given Master Cedric's feedback from your outing, I'm hesitant to add more sexual arts to your studies. Of course, you've only had two classes, so it's possible you could improve in time for Blood Day. But maintaining your virginity is also a trait that many would enjoy bidding on."

I just stared at her. What was I supposed to say to any of that?

"What do you think is the best course, Prospect? Perhaps you weren't quite ready to please a vampire of Master Cedric's caliber, but most who go into the harem industry have to work up to that sort of experience. So this may just be an initial setback. Of course, it's part of your record now, so it may impact placement. Unless you wish to work hard to fix that reputation over the next few months, I mean."

I parted my lips, my voice failing me.

He'd failed me in fighting.

And also in sexual arts?

All he'd done was bite me and please me. Had he expected more? For me to fall to my knees and suck him off?

The vampire was a walking riddle that I couldn't seem to solve!

And now he was destroying my marks in areas I felt sure I could perform in.

Everything he did was meant to undermine me, to make me appear less than my worth. And for what? To be cruel?

"Prospect?" Advisor Livia prompted, her dark brow arching in clear expectation.

"I want to try again," I told her, speaking my mind without thinking it through. "I know I can do better."

She nodded. "All right, then I'll enroll you in the next course. It'll focus more on anal training, as I'd like to keep your vaginal virginity intact for potential use later."

My heart dropped into my stomach. That was not what I'd meant at all. I'd wanted another chance with Master Cedric, not to take the next sexual arts course.

But there was no correcting her now, her long nails were already tapping away at her tablet.

"And what about your fighting course? Would you prefer a different form of exercise?" she asked without looking up at me.

"I want to take the next class," I said automatically, hoping that Master Cedric would be the instructor.

She hummed and keyed in a few notes.

"And obviously we'll continue your service courses since you're excelling there. We'll monitor the weight gain as well, just to make sure this doesn't continue. Otherwise, your food will be adjusted accordingly." She glanced up at me, her green eyes sparkling like emeralds. "I suggest practicing your fighting sequences as much as possible to help with athletic training, in addition to trying to increase your scores in that area."

"Yes, Advisor Livia."

She went back to her notes, humming a little more.

"We'll see how this next round goes, then I may have you partnered again for another off-campus test."

My heart skipped a beat. *With Master Cedric or someone else?* I wondered. But I knew better than to ask. I could only hope he'd be the instructor of my next course, then I could ask him myself.

If I felt brave enough to do so.

He failed me.

Again.

Why?

"Right. I think that's all for this month. Good evening, Prospect." Advisor Livia ended the call before I could say another word, my fate already set.

All I could do was blink blankly at the wall and wonder at my fate.

But the more I stared at the white space, the more resolute I felt.

Master Cedric had doomed me in his course and then called my sexual skills "quite lacking."

He hadn't even given me a chance to properly perform.

I narrowed my gaze, his face suddenly appearing in my mind. *You think I can't please you? Test me properly.* If he wanted to doom me by calling my skills inadequate, then I'd try even harder to prove him wrong.

The first step would be taking an advanced fighting course—one I would pass—and learning more about how to please male vampires.

He might never know. He might not even care. But I did. And I would prove that he was wrong about me.

I wasn't a wilting flower.

I was still Lily. *His* Lily.

Watch me bloom, I thought at Master Cedric, my jaw clenching. *There may not be sunlight here, but I refuse to wither and die. You're wrong about me. You'll see.*

LILY

Seven Months Later

"WE'RE ONE MONTH AWAY FROM BLOOD DAY," ADVISOR Livia informed me as I sat cross-legged on my bed, facing the infamous screen on the wall. "Your scores are exemplary in all your courses."

She started reading them to me as though I didn't know my own grades.

I knew I'd excelled.

I'd pushed myself harder than ever, hoping with each new month that I would see the male who'd doubted my skills and prove to him my worth.

But he'd never appeared.

Master Khalid had taught all the fighting courses.

Including the last one I'd taken that focused on swordsmanship.

And the one before that on archery training.

I'd excelled in both classes, as they were about skill more than physical strength. I'd even outshot Prospect Six Hundred and Forty-Two during the final exam.

Master Cedric appeared to me in my dreams, his

expression never once impressed. So I woke up and tried to prove him wrong again.

And again.

And again.

"We need to discuss the final sexual arts training course," Advisor Livia said, interrupting my thoughts. "I strongly discourage you from taking vaginal training, as your virginity is a high mark in your favor. However, there are, of course, those who prefer skilled females. So if joining a harem is a route that interests you, then we can proceed."

"What are my other options?" I asked, my voice void of emotion.

Because I didn't want to care.

What was the point anyway? I'd practically done everything else to my body except the actual art of traditional intercourse. Why not just complete my training and ensure I was prepared in all ways to serve a master?

Because I still want Master Cedric, I thought darkly. *And some naïve and stupid part of me wants him to be my first. Not Six.*

It didn't matter how many orgasms Six gave me in our sexual arts courses; none of them compared to what Master Cedric had done with his hands.

The ones in class always felt forced, my body reacting because I had no choice.

But Master Cedric had made me feel alive.

Master Cedric is gone. He doesn't care about you. Stop thinking about him, I demanded of myself as Advisor Livia started rattling off course options.

We'd already agreed that I would take the final fighting sequence course.

As well as a class on the food service industry.

And a weekly lesson on pack service requirements, should I end up in a lycan clan.

The last topic was related to sexual arts, which always seemed to be Advisor Livia's favorite regimen to review. She'd restructured my food program again several months ago, cutting back on the increased portions Master Cedric had recommended, but giving me more than my former dietary plan.

It'd allowed me to gain muscle, although not too much.

I felt strong, yet fragile at the same time.

Which she claimed was the perfect combination. Some photos had been taken of me recently to update my records, and she'd been very pleased with my body tone and curves.

So I wasn't surprised at all when she recommended my final course be in the art of pleasing other women. "I think it would give you some versatility," she added, those green eyes of hers glimmering with approval.

"Okay," I agreed, mostly because I preferred that over the other option of vaginal preparedness.

"Excellent," she replied, tapping away at her tablet. "We'll touch base again in two weeks this time, as we are nearing the end of the program and I want to ensure you're prepared. Good evening, Prospect."

She signed off without another word, just like she did at the end of every meeting.

I stared at the wall for a minute, then stood to prepare for my classes.

The water in my closet had helped me through the last eight months, but I was down to my last seven bottles. I left them alone, saving them for a day when I needed them most.

Part of me still believed Master Cedric had put them there. It was the same part of me that dreamt of him every night.

I'd only known him for a handful of weeks. And most

of those days had been spent in class where I'd tried to please him and he'd constantly failed me.

Then we'd spent one powerful night together.

That was it.

Yet his presence in my life had impacted me more than anyone else ever had. And I couldn't figure out how to erase him from my mind.

The only positive that came from the experience was my obsession with proving him wrong. Because in the process of doing so, I'd managed to nearly perfect my scores.

My door beeped as the latch unbolted. Then a schedule rolled across my wall as Advisor Livia sent me my revised course information. As per usual after every monthly meeting, my lesson times and locations would change immediately.

Sometimes one or two courses would stay mostly the same, such as my introductory fighting course with Master Cedric that had gone on for more than a one-month term. At least until Master Khalid had taken over. Then it'd become his course that had continued, but the name and purpose had changed every month after that.

But this time, everything on my schedule shifted.

I studied the revised regimen and committed the details to memory.

Then I went through my usual routine of showering and picking up breakfast.

Two scoops of eggs. A full piece of toast. Half of a banana.

Almost the same as yesterday, just a different type of fruit today. Yesterday was half of an apple.

I ate quickly, finished a quarter of my water, and went to the food services course.

Master Clarissa was in charge again, which didn't surprise me. She tended to lead these types of classes.

The majority of the students involved were the same as well, including Six. I stood beside him like I usually did when we had a course together and listened as Master Clarissa explained our first task.

My clan organization course was next—Six didn't attend this one with me—which was led by a lycan named Master Felix. He didn't appear all that thrilled to be teaching, his gruff tone and scowl clear markers of his annoyance.

And he dismissed us early.

I used the time to drop my new books off in my room and eat the protein bar I'd received for lunch.

Then I headed toward the gymnasium building for my new fighting course. Advisor Livia had said this final regimen would combine several tools together from the previous classes.

I hoped that meant I could use a bow again.

It'd been fun to aim at targets.

Even though they'd been shaped like human bodies with the bull's-eye being the heart.

Master Khalid was already in the room when I arrived, his attention on his tablet. He wore his trademark black jeans and a matching T-shirt—an outfit he chose to wear to every class for the last eight months—giving him an intimidating appearance.

I'd originally assumed he was a lycan because of his height and muscular arms.

But he was actually a vampire.

Something I'd discovered when he'd drunk a glass of blood wine during one of our exams. His gaze had turned predatory at the time, reminding me of Master Cedric.

Fortunately, I hadn't been the one on the receiving end of that look.

Prospect One Hundred and Thirty-Nine had been the one he'd eyed with interest. She'd finally recovered from her injuries—something that had taken several weeks—and had been my partner in these courses ever since.

His gaze went to her now as she entered, the blues of his irises seeming to overtake the green. Then he blinked and went back to his tablet.

She scurried up beside me to set her items down next to mine. There were floor mats in the center of the room, suggesting we would be sparring again. But neither of us took off our shoes yet. We would once Master Khalid confirmed today's task.

The archery courses had started in this same room before he'd led us outside. So it was possible he'd do something similar today.

More prospects entered the room, many of them familiar, but not from my previous fighting courses.

Actually, aside from me and Prospect One Hundred and Thirty-Nine, only two others were participants from our last course.

Odd.

We all usually progressed as a unit.

Perhaps our group was joining another class?

But if that was the case, where were all of our other former classmates?

Six entered, his eyes immediately meeting mine. A note of confusion flickered in his light green eyes. I responded in kind.

He joined me and Prospect One Hundred and Thirty-Nine and set his bag beside mine. "What course name do you have right now?" he asked in a low tone.

"Advanced Fighting Session Seven," I whispered back to him. "You?"

"Advanced Endurance Session Seven." His gaze met mine as he added the location and time.

"Same as mine, but a different name," I replied.

Others in the class had begun to murmur as well, causing Master Khalid to clear his throat. "Quiet."

Everyone fell silent immediately.

Minutes passed, and more prospects entered until there were nearly sixty or seventy of us.

Something is very wrong, I thought, swallowing.

Most of my classes had ten to fifteen humans, max.

Several of us exchanged glances, the nerves palpable. I did my best to remain neutral, but it became harder to mask my reaction as more and more prospects arrived—all of them ones I recognized as being in my year.

Six's arm brushed mine, his knuckles sweeping across the back of my hand. I didn't look at him, but I returned the gesture. We weren't friends. Just allies. We'd been through a lot together, and sometimes we attempted to share comfort in the other's presence.

This was one of those times.

I started counting the prospects, needing a distraction, but only reached seventy-two when Master Khalid started speaking.

"Tonight's course will take place in a new arena outside the university gates," he announced. "I'll lead you to the exit. Your objective is to run and use whatever skills you have to survive, and try not to die when you're caught."

Master Khalid started toward the door in a casual saunter, acting as though he hadn't just handed us all a death sentence in the span of seconds.

Six's hand twitched against mine.

I nearly grabbed his palm in response.

But I was too frozen to move.

Run. Fight. Try not to die when caught.

Master Khalid's instructions reverberated through my mind, the words making me cold inside.

But he didn't give any of us time to fully process his command.

Because that wasn't how vampires and lycans worked. They expected immediate obedience.

"Now, Prospects," Master Khalid snapped, his tone lined with impatience.

Prospect One Hundred and Thirty-Nine flinched, then stepped forward as though his voice had yanked her into action. Master Khalid glanced at her, his turquoise eyes gleaming with hunger. It was how he usually looked at her. But he never acted on it.

However, something told me he might tonight.

And her brittle steps suggested she suspected that, too.

There wasn't anything I could do to help her. Just like I couldn't truly console Six, either.

We were all in this world on our own. Most of us wouldn't survive for long.

And it seemed tonight's exercise would be driving that home more than any other.

A solemn air swirled around us as we all followed Master Khalid down the hallway, out the door of our building, and along the wall outside.

It didn't escape my notice that the majority of the bulky males from my fighting course sequence were missing. Most of the female prospects around me also rivaled my height and size.

And the males were all larger and similar in stature to Six.

He was over six feet tall and athletically lean, which

probably made him fast on his feet. Perhaps that was what he'd focused on in his endurance courses.

Had I made a mistake by taking fighting sequences instead?

I could move quickly in most situations. But I wasn't sure how long or how fast I could run.

"And try not to die when you're caught," Master Khalid had said.

Those words haunted my mind with each step. *Who are we running from? What do they intend to do to us after they catch us?*

Maybe this was an exercise for the Vigils, a way to keep them sharp and test our merits against them. That was what I'd been training for all these months.

However, that didn't explain Six and the others joining us now.

Nor did it explain the weapons scattered all over the ground beside a pair of large wooden doors ahead of us. They weren't the same ones I'd ventured through with Master Cedric all those months ago. They were pedestrian-sized instead and etched into the side of a nearby guard tower.

The Vigils on top all watched us with vacant looks, their body language exuding boredom more than anticipation.

So this isn't for them, I translated, swallowing.

Of course, I'd already suspected that.

A Vigil exercise would have included more of the men from my previous courses.

This was something else.

Something bad.

Master Khalid stopped before reaching the mess of weapons, his gaze flicking over us as he turned and waited for everyone to catch up.

We'd formed a natural line along the concrete walkway that bordered the massive university walls.

A long, sandy courtyard decorated the other half of the path. The university buildings were beyond it, the structures all boxy and cream-colored, just like the wall surrounding the campus.

Six shivered beside me, his knuckles brushing mine in that need for comfort.

I returned the gesture.

But once this game started, we would be on our own. For better or for worse.

The crescent moon cast ominous shadows across Master Khalid's chiseled features, accentuating the eerie promise hanging in the air.

This is going to hurt.

His expression gave nothing away. And neither did his voice as he said, "Pick a tool."

A tool, not a weapon.

An interesting distinction, considering the items on the ground.

Prospect One Hundred and Thirty-Nine was the first to move. Her choice of a set of throwing stars didn't surprise me. She often nailed her target with those during our weapons training course.

Others moved to make their own selections, followed by me and Six. It became more of an orderly ordeal since we'd all fallen automatically into this line.

Fortunately, Six and I were near the front.

He chose a hammer.

I picked up a pair of daggers.

The bow and quiver of arrows beside it would have been my first choice if it were daytime. But I wanted a close-range "tool" for this course assignment—something I could use to protect myself when "caught."

Master Khalid observed as the rest of the prospects filed through to claim their items.

I stood off to the side between my usual sparring partner and Six. Tension radiated off of them, blanketing me in a static energy that hummed through my very being.

I shivered, and it had nothing to do with the climate. I couldn't even feel the air around me. Master Khalid claimed my focus, his pending command—whatever it would be—becoming my entire world.

The doors behind him opened to reveal the sandy plains beyond the walls.

Nothing for miles and miles.

Except for a royal palace, I reminded myself.

But we were facing a different part of the desert. I didn't know which direction to run in to find Master Cedric's home. I wasn't even sure he'd be there.

Besides, what would I do? Casually knock on his door and ask for safety?

I nearly snorted at the concept.

He hadn't shown an inkling of interest in me since his goodbye kiss.

He wasn't even here tonight.

Yet my obsession with him nagged at my mind, making me consider the option of running to him.

How would he react? Would he leave me in the sand to die? That might be the goal of this game anyway. So perhaps I should try to find him.

Run and survive.

Fight when you're caught.

The thoughts were my own voice but reminiscent of Master Khalid's explanation for tonight's class.

He clasped his hands now, his posture utterly relaxed. "You get a five-minute head start. Then the hunt begins." He stepped aside, giving us free access to the doors. "*Run.*"

LILY

A THUNDEROUS GUNSHOT RIPPED THROUGH THE AIR FROM above, the sound deafening.

And then everyone started running.

Feet pounding. Sand flying. The world whirling in a blur of motion that I couldn't decipher.

Because I was among them, sprinting through the doors and out into unexplored lands.

I turned on instinct, my mind struggling to remember the direction of Master Cedric's home.

It was an insane plan. A notion I should squash. But that one night with him had provided me with a dose of safety I now craved.

Another crack of thunder rattled the earth. Or maybe it was my violent tremble that made it feel as though the ground moved beneath my feet.

That doesn't mean five minutes are up, right? I wondered. It felt as though only a few seconds had passed, a minute at most.

I didn't debate it.

I just kept sprinting through the desert, the walls of the university staying within sight. *The road,* I thought breathlessly. *If I can find the road, I can follow it.*

The rest of that plan didn't exist in my brain. Survival was my only goal.

I clutched the handles of my knives as I pushed myself harder, needing to find the road.

Pavement.

Leading into the darkness.

Illuminated only by the moon.

I recalled the details I could remember, but they were fuzzy at best.

Boom.

Was that the third one? Three minutes? Four minutes?

My heart was beating so loudly in my ears that I couldn't even be sure I'd heard the appropriate amount of gunshots. Dizziness and exertion weighed me down, my body unprepared for this sprint into the darkness.

I should have paced myself.

My pulse raced, my lungs screaming for air.

I didn't run often enough. I wasn't going to make it.

What's going to pursue me? What will happen when whatever it is catches me?

The loud clap of sound went off again, making me jump and nearly lose my footing. I couldn't see anything aside from the wall and desert. No road. No end in sight.

I went the wrong way, I realized.

But there was no turning back now.

I had to push. To run. To find a place to hide and defend myself. But where? In a sand mound?

I nearly laughed. Yet I couldn't push out enough oxygen for the sound to form.

Run. Run. Run.

I took off away from the wall, searching for anything that could provide me with shelter.

There were no other prospects nearby. At least none that I could hear or see.

Had any of them joined forces to fight together?

Which direction had Six gone in? What about my course partner?

Don't think about them. Worry about finding a place to hide, I coached myself, my palms slickening with sweat.

I'd endured some intense exams before. But nothing compared to this. Not even Master Cedric's sparring assignment with that prospect who had broken my arm.

A final bullet hit the air. Or I thought it might have been final. I'd lost count what felt like forever ago.

Funny how time seemed long now. Yet unfairly short, too.

A scream echoed through the night, making my blood run cold. *It's started.*

A shriek followed.

Oh, Goddess…

I was running in the middle of nothing, searching for a place that didn't exist!

A road that I would never find.

A palace that I'd reached by *car*, not by running.

This was a terrible plan.

I froze.

Then hunched down.

I needed a new objective. A new way to win this.

The knives felt slippery in my hands, but I clutched them as though they were my sole purpose in life.

Calm, I whispered to myself. *Calm your breaths. Focus and listen.*

More screams and shouts littered the night, their proximity unknown due to the open space. They sounded far away but likely weren't.

I stole a deep breath, my palms tightening in expectation.

Survive when caught.

I could do that.

I *would* do that.

I just had to wait.

There was nowhere to run here. Nowhere to hide. I was destined to be captured, the land too flat and dark and vastly sparse to provide any semblance of escape.

Anyone trying to do otherwise would be disappointed.

I shouldn't have wasted time searching for the road. I knew better. But my body had reacted as though Master Cedric had yanked me to him on a string.

My obsession with him was going to cost me my life.

I shifted into a fighting pose, preparing for the inevitable. Then I waited, my breathing slowing back to normal with each passing second.

This felt right.

I needed my strength and focus, not the adrenaline provoked by the run.

More shouts arose, one of them sounding suspiciously like Six.

But I didn't react.

Instead, I continued to breathe. Waiting. Concentrating. *Listening.*

The desert was eerily silent, the wind nonexistent. The only disruptions were human cries.

I listened for footsteps and signs of movement.

Nothing.

My heart skipped a beat, my insides threatening to melt beneath the pressure of the moment.

However, I forced myself to inhale and exhale, using all my lessons to calm my body despite the burning desire to run and scream.

I could almost taste the agony of the others in the air, their whimpers echoing in the still night.

I'm next. They'll be here soon. Just wait.

But the inevitable merely made it worse.

I started to count to distract my mind.

It didn't work. I couldn't stop picturing the violence occurring around me. Hearing it was almost worse than seeing it. And knowing I would be next…

I swallowed.

My eyes nearly closed. *If I can't see it happening, it won't be real.*

But it was *very* real.

As evidenced by the shadow strolling toward me.

A leisurely walk.

A canter that captivated my attention and had me tightening my grip on my blades.

It's my turn.

I'd expected the being to charge at me. To attack. But it merely walked toward me with a lazy pace that drew out the moment.

"Are you going to stab me, little flower?"

The deep, accented voice chased away my instincts, causing me to nearly drop my knives.

Master Cedric.

Or was my mind playing tricks on me? Causing me to morph this dark game into one I might enjoy?

The shadow was nearly before me, the moon illuminating his back instead of his front.

Is it him? Is it really Master Cedric?

"Did you fail to understand tonight's objective, sweetling?" He pitched his voice low, whisper-soft, the accent now disguised.

It's not him.

I imagined it.

I need to—

He caught me by the throat. "*Survive*," he told me, the anger in his voice forcing me into action.

This wasn't Master Cedric. I'd dreamt up his voice and presence. Because I couldn't let him go. The vampire haunted me, even during waking hours.

Fight, I coached myself, my hands flicking as I attempted to stab him. He rotated away from me, releasing my neck.

But he was too fast.

Too strong.

Too *skilled*.

His hand caught my wrist, twisting it and forcing me to release one blade. It was my weaker hand, so I didn't bother trying to stop the movement.

Instead, I concentrated on my good hand and my aim, my arm lifting in an arc that would allow me to stab the assailant in the chest.

He dodged it, his feet taking him off to the side. Then he attempted to grab me again. But I ducked, my eyes having acclimated enough to the dark to perceive his shadow.

He chuckled, the sound a taunt. Because it sounded like Master Cedric. Except it wasn't him. It couldn't be him.

I jumped back as he attempted to grab me once more.

Then I made the only move I could by throwing my blade when he attempted to capture me a third time.

He blurred in response, his shadow phasing around to my back to catch me in a bruising grip.

The air whooshed from my lungs as his palm grasped my throat again, his opposite arm snaking around my waist to hold me against him.

"Ah, my sweet Lily flower," he breathed against my ear,

the familiar name making me gasp. "What have you done?"

My back hit the sand in the next instant as Master Cedric took me to the ground in a swift, harsh movement.

He caught my wrists in one hand and tugged my arms over my head to pin them. Then his opposite hand went to my cheek, his touch surprisingly gentle.

The moon cast his face in ominous shadows, but this close, there was no mistaking his identity.

Master Cedric is here.

On top of me.

Pinning me against the ground.

And he looks furious.

The anger resembled black flames in his dark irises, causing me to shiver beneath him.

Or maybe it was just feeling him against my skin that elicited the tremble.

I went from fighting for my survival to being a willing captive in mere seconds.

A stupid reaction.

Yet I couldn't fight him. I was too elated to see him again after all this time. *My Master Cedric.*

"Tell me, darling, do you understand the purpose of this course?" His low, silky tones spread goose bumps down my arms.

"Training," I whispered. But I didn't know what we were training for. Because this had nothing to do with becoming a Vigil.

He hummed, the sound telling me I hadn't answered correctly.

"Training for what, though, is the question." His nose skimmed my cheekbone. "This is an arena where the prospects run and the Masters chase. It's a game my peers look forward to every year. Because once we catch our desired prey, we can do whatever we want to make it scream. The whole point is to see how long it takes until the human breaks."

A chill skated down my spine, chasing away the warmth his presence had evoked.

A game of chase and capture and torture.

An arena where Masters can catch and torment prospects.

It didn't surprise me at all that Master Cedric had chosen me for that purpose. He had been taunting me from the beginning, failing me at every turn.

And now would be no different at all.

"Tell me what you're being trained to do," he said, his voice holding a lethal edge to it.

"To be chased and caught." The reply automatically left me as though he controlled my mind, body, and tongue.

"By what?"

"You," I whispered.

He smiled, but it didn't appear to be all that kind. "No, darling. *Lycans.*"

My lips parted. "Moon chase…" The words were barely audible, but his responding nod told me he'd heard them just fine.

"Yes. Tonight's exercise is about testing your merit for a moon chase. And do you know what lycans love?" His thumb stroked my wrist, the touch deceptively tender.

I tried to speak, but I couldn't even manage to swallow. I was too busy processing the concept of tonight's test.

For the first time, I didn't want to pass.

I didn't know much about the moon chase, but I knew enough about the requirements—run until caught. Then die.

It was a game for the lycans, a way to play with their prey.

Vampires were given walking blood slaves. Lycans were given prey to hunt.

"They like a fight," Master Cedric continued when I didn't reply. "They adore prey that doesn't submit. And sexually skilled prey is even better. Because the harder a human works, the more aroused a lycan becomes."

He pressed his groin into the apex between my thighs, allowing me to feel his own interest.

It branded me even through our clothes, eliciting a whimper from my lips.

He tsked. "You're exactly the kind of prey a lycan will take as a temporary pet. A human to indulge his needs until the next moon chase. If you're lucky, you'll die quickly in his care. If you're unlucky, he'll use you until your spirit is broken and then send you to a breeding camp."

Tears threatened my eyes at the brutal future he'd just described.

That fate was worse than a harem. Worse than the service industry. Worse than anything else imaginable in this world.

"Continuing the fighting courses after I failed you only proves you have spirit. And your sexual aptitude marks are quite impressive, too. Now you're among the last of the humans to scream during this exercise. What do you think all that means, little flower?"

I stopped breathing, the realization strangling me from the inside out.

I'd been training all this time for the moon chase. Not to be a Vigil. Not to join a harem. But to become a temporary human pet to a lycan.

Ice drizzled through my veins.

And the world around me began to sway.

"A spirited human with a virgin pussy," Master Cedric

drawled, his words doing nothing to thaw my frigid interior. His tongue clicked at me, the sound reminding me of a ticking time bomb.

I couldn't believe I'd wanted to run toward him, that I'd been craving his touch all these months.

He was a monster.

A monster who was clearly enjoying my torment now.

Because he was *chuckling* at my response.

Except the sound didn't come off as amused. It was too harsh for that.

"You know, I don't typically enjoy this annual event, little flower. I usually just track down a random human and break a bone to make the prospect scream. But I'm rather enjoying drawing this out with you."

Of course he was enjoying this. He always enjoyed torturing me.

Was that why he'd taken me to his palace? To give me a day of hope to hang over my head for months in glorious agony?

His lips whispered across mine, his desire still pressing intimately against me.

But my body didn't respond the way it would have mere moments ago.

I was too cold now, too... too *infuriated*... to indulge in it. Because he'd taken everything away—ripped away the false beliefs from my soul and used that residual hope to pierce my heart.

I felt shredded.

Dead.

Yet furious at the same time.

His tongue traced my lip, a hum of approval coming from him. "Now you get it," he murmured. "Now you see your purpose."

Hatred unfurled inside my being, shooting sparks of

warmth through my veins as his tongue slid into my mouth.

I bit down on instinct, wanting him to feel even a fraction of the pain he'd caused.

His blood trickled into my throat, but I didn't swallow. I spat it back at him instead as I began to squirm beneath him.

I didn't want to be pinned down. I didn't want another moment of this torment. I wanted to *kill* him.

He'd set me up in the worst way.

And he was enjoying my inevitable misery now.

"I hate you," I seethed, my words low and hoarse from what felt like hours of being unable to swallow. But I ignored all that now. I no longer had anything left to lose. If the moon chase was my fate, why bother trying to please anyone anymore?

I preferred death to becoming a lycan's pet.

I preferred death to allowing Master Cedric another moment of amusement at my expense.

I preferred death to all of this bullshit.

So I fought him in earnest, bucking my hips and trying with all my might to dislodge him.

His palm claimed my throat, giving it a squeeze.

I dared him to do it by lifting my head off the ground and moving into his death grip. Then I thrashed my arms and legs, uncaring of my training. Uncaring of anything other than ending all this now.

His mouth claimed mine again.

So I bit his lip.

His blood taunted my tongue.

But I didn't want it. I used the remaining saliva in my mouth to dislodge it against his face.

He growled.

And I growled back.

Because what the hell did I have to lose? He'd just subjected me to a lifetime of agony.

Fuck. That.

His palm squeezed. "*Enough.*"

"Fuck you," I mouthed back at him, fully aware that using those words was forbidden for humankind. But enough lycans and vampires used them in my presence for me to know what they meant.

"Lily," he snapped.

"Not my name," I reminded him on a wheeze, my lungs crying out from a lack of oxygen.

But still I didn't care.

I fought.

He held me down with ease, his stronger form dominating mine.

It was futile.

However, I couldn't seem to stop. I wanted to murder him. He'd done this to me. He'd set me up. And for what? Some sick satisfaction in watching me wither and die?

"Stop," he commanded.

I ignored him.

He'd lost his ability to control me when he'd decided to reveal his true intentions. All of this had been meant to groom me for the moon chase.

I wanted to scream. But his grip prevented the sound from escaping.

Right. Because he wanted me to finally pass a test—*this* test. The humans who didn't break quickly would be rated highly.

I almost laughed at the insanity of the situation. All I had wanted for months was another chance to please him and prove my worth.

Well, I'd gotten my wish.

Because I was more than excelling at this challenge.

A tear escaped my eye, the treacherous droplet revealing just how broken I felt by this revelation.

One month until Blood Day.

One month until the Magistrate sealed my fate.

One month until the real chase began.

And there was nothing I could do to stop it.

Nothing I could do to save myself.

I closed my eyes, the fight leaving my limbs as my lungs wept with the need to breathe.

But even as Master Cedric released my throat, I fought the urge to inhale.

Because I no longer wanted to survive.

Not with the moon chase being my fate.

I'd played all my cards wrong.

And now all I had left was a losing hand.

"Lily," Master Cedric whispered.

I continued to ignore him.

There was no one here by that name.

Just Prospect Four Hundred and Seven.

Destined for the moon chase.

Maybe I would be lucky, like he'd said. Maybe the lycans would kill me quickly. But when had my life ever been about luck?

Master Cedric's palm returned to my cheek. "Oh, sweet flower." His forehead met mine. "Don't wilt."

I nearly grunted. But that sound required air, and I refused to allow it for that purpose alone.

He'd wanted to destroy me.

And he'd won.

All I could do now was accept the inevitable.

I finally let myself breathe.

And then I screamed.

Ending the game once and for all.

CEDRIC

Fuck.

The broken quality of Lily's scream would haunt me for eternity. It was worse than I'd feared, my infatuation with her having pierced a part of me that very few had ever reached.

It'd taken every ounce of my strength not to check up on her over the last eight months. But it was the only way to finish Silvano's task—which I'd wrapped up last week.

When I'd returned to the university yesterday, I'd been expecting to find my little flower safely sequestered in servant-focused courses.

Alas, no. The stubborn little brat had continued taking fighting sequences and sexual studies, thus driving home her fate.

A fate I'd felt compelled to lay out for her plainly tonight because I was livid.

I'd failed her with purpose—to protect her. And she'd disregarded all of it, walking straight into the moon chase trap.

Even tonight, she'd reacted perfectly for such a fate by standing her ground and trying to fight.

The wolves were going to rip her apart and fuck her in a puddle of her own blood.

Just the notion of it made my blood boil all over again.

So yeah, I'd reacted harshly.

But never in my wildest dreams had I imagined she'd respond in this way—fighting me one minute and screaming in the next.

Her eyes were closed now, but I'd seen the color dull in her gaze before she'd shut me out completely.

Wilting. Drying up. Dying right beneath me.

It was the nightmare I'd feared, the reality I'd known I would one day face. I just hadn't expected it to be tonight. Not when I'd finally made it back to her.

I released her wrists, both my palms caressing her cheeks.

She didn't react other than to lie there and continue to scream. The sound was scratchy now, her throat too damaged to function the way she desired.

"Lily," I breathed, my thumbs tracing the hollows beneath her eyes.

Fuck, I'd missed her more than anyone else I could ever remember missing.

Being away from her had been agony. I'd finished the job as quickly as I could, my need to return to her a driving force behind every decision.

I should have checked up on her.

Except there was nothing I could have done, no way to communicate and warn her away from this path.

Maybe I could have explained my necessary absence, told her bluntly to avoid those courses. But there hadn't been time for that conversation. And I hadn't wanted to risk her mentioning anything to the wrong person—like her "advisor."

Lily's scream cracked as her throat gave out on her

entirely. She went completely limp beneath me, awaiting her fate. But this was a game she didn't fully understand.

I'd caught her.

That made her my prize.

Several others were playing with their new toys out in the desert. It was meant to be an introduction to the future and the fates that awaited them.

But I had a different plan for Lily.

A plan that had not begun the way I'd originally hoped. I'd fix it. Just not here.

I rolled off of her and up to my feet. "Stand up."

She merely lay there, her breaths shallow, her pulse slow. It was like she'd decided to die right here, right now.

Except she wasn't injured in any way that would allow for it. I knew this because I had been the one to take her down.

Anyone else would have made her bleed.

Instead, she'd made *me* bleed.

And then she'd spat out my blood as though it were foul and beneath her.

My gaze narrowed at the reminder. I could feel the evidence of her reaction hardening against my chin.

Any other situation, and I'd force her to lick it off.

But this current predicament required a different kind of approach. So I used the sleeve of my dark, long-sleeved dress shirt to scrub the evidence off instead.

Lily remained unmoving on the ground, my command clearly doing nothing for her.

"So that's what it's going to be? I give you a little bit of truth, and you shut down?" I stared down at her, waiting for a reply.

Nothing.

It was like she couldn't even hear me.

I knelt and pressed my palm to her abdomen. She'd

filled out a little over the last few months, her increased food regimen helping her curves.

Of course, her "advisor" had still cut down on the recommendations I'd written down before leaving.

Just as she'd disregarded my suggestions for service work and instead allowed Lily to continue her fighting and sexual course tracks.

It hadn't surprised me at all to see a female-oral class added to her courses for this final round.

Too bad for Livia, Lily wouldn't be taking that course.

In fact, she was done with all her classes.

I ran my fingers up her torso, going to the bruises now forming on her throat. I'd gripped her too hard, something my anger and enhanced strength had influenced. I bent to kiss her neck, vowing to make it better.

Then I pressed my lips to her ear. "We get one month together, Lily. One month where you're mine. Now get up so I can take you home."

Well, not my real home. But back to my temporary one.

I'd planned tonight perfectly, ensuring I captured the prize I desired and, for once, taking advantage of my right to claim a prospect.

It happened often at the Blood Universities. No one cared. It was viewed as a benefit to being stuck in these godforsaken areas and devoting our time to training human slaves.

But none of the prospects had ever appealed to me before. Not until Lily.

Except she still didn't react, her body seeming to go cold beneath my touch.

Frowning, I pulled back to examine her.

"I know you're awake," I told her. "I know you can hear me."

Her eyes opened then, the color of her irises so dull that I nearly flinched. She resembled death, her spirit utterly broken. "I don't want to play anymore." The words were barely audible, her throat so thoroughly abused from her screams and my hands that she couldn't speak.

"Hmm. Well, that's too bad, little flower, because I came back here to play with you." I bit my wrist and pressed it to her mouth. "Drink."

There weren't cameras out here.

And my night vision told me no one was close enough to see or hear our conversation.

It wasn't necessarily safe, but we didn't have a choice.

Lily clenched her jaw, refusing my blood.

So I pinched her chin with my opposite hand and forced her lips to part.

Her nostrils flared.

"Drink or I'm going to suffocate you," I warned. I wouldn't actually do it. But I would find a way to force her to swallow.

Her pale eyes flashed, the first sign of life returning to her features.

Then she bit my wrist.

Hard.

I smiled. "Is that your version of a punishment?" I released her jaw to run my knuckles across her cheek. "Because I consider biting to be foreplay, sweetling."

She growled, her hands flying up off the ground as she tried to scratch me or slap me or *something.* It wasn't a thought-out attack; it was desperate and a little sad.

However, I allowed her one slap.

Then I caught her wrists and pulled them together against her chest to hold them with one palm.

Her expression turned feral as she tried to fight again.

LEXI C. FOSS

I cupped her cheek and kissed her, grateful to see her spirit once more.

Then I pulled back when she tried to bite me again, and instead pressed my wrist to her mouth once more.

She bit down, only seeming to belatedly realize that was exactly what I wanted.

She tried to rotate her head to dislodge my wrist, but I followed her with ease before applying some pressure to hold her in place. "Swallow and I'll let you go."

Blue fire licked through her irises, overcoming the green.

It was a gorgeous sight watching her come back to life. This time, I would give her the roots she needed to stay alive.

She swallowed, all the while staring me down and hating me with her gaze.

I could accept that hatred. I much preferred it to her deathlike expression from moments ago.

"Again," I said, mostly just to stoke the flames of her fury.

She'd completely broken out of her prospect mode, allowing me to see the soul beneath the beaten exterior.

And I very much liked what I saw.

Her throat worked as she complied. Then she swallowed a third and a fourth time before I could command it.

Lily's cheeks blossomed with color, her eyes vibrant once more.

Beautiful.

I slowly took my wrist from her mouth. "Good girl."

She snorted. "Fuck you."

My lips curled. "Your vocabulary has improved since the last time we spoke." I settled back on my knees beside her and released her wrists. "I'm curious to find out what else has improved."

She lunged upward, leading with her fist. I caught her hand and yanked her into me.

"And your fighting skills have *not* improved." Although, her aim with that dagger earlier had been rather deadly.

She squirmed, the battle between us reignited by my words. Her elbow shot upward toward my jaw, causing me to release her wrist, as the position put her at risk for an injury.

But she mistook my movement as a win.

And attempted to go full force at my face again.

"Okay." I grabbed a fistful of her hair, yanked her head back, and bit her.

She shrieked in response, her hands landing on my shoulders as she attempted to shove me away.

But within seconds, her push became a pull as her lips parted from the euphoria in my bite.

"I hate you," she breathed, but the words lacked conviction as her body swayed to my vampiric command.

I wrapped my opposite arm around her, holding her to me as I drank deeply from her vein. Her essence resembled a drug to my senses, my body having gone too long without her flavor.

Fuck, I was addicted to this female. My sweet, beautiful flower.

What was it about her that captivated me so entirely that I was willing to rush Silvano's task just to return to her? She'd been my goal, *my reward*, that'd helped me through my mission.

I'd been so looking forward to our reunion.

My plan had been to steal her away in the middle of the night from here and make her my personal servant for the month.

Then I'd seen her schedule—found *this* course waiting for her tonight—and my strategy had immediately shifted.

She would still be going home with me.

We would still have our month.

But now I had to find a way to alter her path. Because the moon chase could not be her future. I refused to allow it.

"Master Cedric," she moaned, that voice going straight to my groin and igniting my need for more.

We'd only just begun our journey together. Then Silvano had robbed us of what precious little time we had left.

Eight months felt like nothing to one my age.

Yet those months had stretched on for what felt like an eternity.

I guided her back to the ground again with my fangs embedded in her throat.

She writhed in response, her legs automatically parting in blatant invitation. I settled between her thighs, my hand leaving her hair to move downward and cup her breast.

Much better, I thought, pleased with her body's natural response to receiving proper meals.

She arched into me, completely lost to my bite and the endorphins flooding her system.

Another needy little sound left her throat.

I reveled in it and smiled as I sensed another vampire approaching us. He would have heard the slip in her conditioning. That would benefit me when I stated my desire to keep her for a month.

Unless he chose to take her himself.

But I doubted he would.

I'd seen his interest in another.

I lifted my gaze to find him only ten feet away with that particular female in his arms, her body lifeless.

However, the hint of a pulse told me she was still alive. *Barely.*

"Are you going to kill her?" His deep voice made Lily freeze beneath me. She would recognize it since he'd been her instructor these last few months. "Because I think that would be a waste."

The warning in his tone was unexpected.

Prince Khalid wasn't one to care about frivolous deaths. He was a renowned assassin, after all.

When I'd called him with the news about Silvano's demand, he'd told me he would take care of temporarily reassigning my classes. The university bordered his region, making it his responsibility to oversee.

But I'd been rather stunned to find out he'd flown in to personally cover the classes in my absence. I'd expected him to delegate the task.

However, his name on the schedule read as *Master Khalid,* not *Prince Khalid,* which left me wondering what game he was playing here.

He wasn't like other royals. He tended to do his own thing and lurk in the shadows.

So if he was here, he was here for a reason.

And I really did not want to intrude on his plans.

I carefully released Lily's neck and went to my knees between her spread thighs, purposefully holding myself in an inferior position to him as a show of respect.

"It would be a waste," I agreed with him, referring back to his comments regarding ending Lily's life.

He studied me for a beat. "Then she's released?"

"No. I'm claiming her for the month."

His dark eyebrows rose. "Oh?"

"Is that going to be a problem?"

"Not at all," he replied. "The palace could use more life."

A subtle reminder that he was staying there now as well. And his bloodline made him my superior, too. Which meant I would have to share her when he asked.

I dipped my chin in acknowledgment of his unspoken threat.

He returned the gesture. "Let's plan to have evening breakfast. I believe we have certain things to discuss. Eight o'clock sharp will do."

"Yes, My—"

"Enjoy your night," he interjected, strolling away before I could deliver the formal acceptance of his request.

I stared after him, then glanced down to find Lily lying perfectly still beneath me. Her wide eyes were filled with a thousand questions.

And underlined with just a smidge of hatred.

I could work with that.

"Will you stand up with me now?" I asked. "Or do I need to pick you up?"

She lifted a shaking hand to her neck and the puncture wounds that had not yet healed. "I'll stand."

I moved to my feet first, brushed the sand off my pants, and then waited for her to follow. She was slow but managed to find her balance after a few seconds of wobbling.

Then she tried to shake off the sand clinging to her clothes and hair and nearly fell again.

I caught her by the hip and used my opposite hand to help her. She gritted her teeth but didn't comment. And the look didn't abate even as I combed my fingers through her long golden hair.

"You'll need a shower to get it all off of you," I said softly.

She didn't reply. Instead, she closed her eyes for a beat

and shivered. Her pale skin indicated that she was feeling the effects of her blood loss.

And the open wounds on her neck probably weren't helping.

I gently pulled her closer and pressed my mouth to the bite mark. She gasped, her hands finding my shoulders for balance.

I sliced my tongue and ran it across the indentations, then I took her mouth and forced her to swallow some of my essence.

She didn't fight me this time.

Nor did she bite me.

She merely accepted my kiss without returning it.

I grinned, liking this new challenge in her. "We're going to have fun together, little flower."

"You mean *you* are going to have fun," she corrected, the fierceness in her tone surprising me.

I grasped the back of her nape, forcing her to meet my gaze. "No, sweet flower. It's *we*. You'll see."

She narrowed her gaze. "I don't want to play."

"As I said already, that's really too bad. Because I came back to this hellhole specifically to play with you. And I have no intention of changing my plans."

LILY

"Follow me, Prospect. One step out of line and I'll assume that means you prefer to be carried." Master Cedric's words wrapped around me like a noose, yanking me forward as though he held the end of my leash.

Mostly because I was too busy processing his earlier words to fight my instinct to obey.

"I came back to this hellhole specifically to play with you."

He'd mentioned that once before as well, but it hadn't really registered until his last comment.

If he hadn't been here, then where had he gone?

And why had he returned for me?

Did *torture* mean *play* in his warped vampire mind?

"I'm claiming her for the month."

That was what he'd said to Master Khalid. *What does that even mean?*

I nearly asked now, but we were already by a side door of the wall. Master Cedric pressed his finger to a panel, causing a series of beeps to register before the door hissed open.

It wasn't like the doors we'd used to exit into the desert.

This one was a single entryway with only a foot of clearance over Master Cedric's head.

And it opened into a stairway that led downward, not to the courtyard.

Master Cedric stepped inside with a gesture for me to follow.

The air-conditioning hit me full force, nearly toppling me with the abrupt temperature change. It was unlike anything I'd experienced in the buildings here.

I started to tremble, my fighting clothes too thin for this environment.

Master Cedric didn't seem to notice, his steps clipped as he led the way downward.

I jumped as the door sealed behind me, then skipped forward to catch up to him, my teeth already beginning to chatter. I tried to stop them, aware that displaying such a humanlike reaction would infuriate him, but I couldn't seem to stop the shudder working through me.

His blood wasn't helping.

My senses were heightening more and more with each passing second, making the air down here almost unbearable. Each inhale felt like knives prickling my lungs.

Master Cedric stopped abruptly at the bottom, his dark gaze assessing as he glanced back at me.

I almost apologized.

Except my tongue resembled an ice block.

His eyes narrowed. "You're cold." Not a question, but a statement.

I blinked.

He grabbed me in the next second, lifting me into his arms and cradling me against his chest.

And then we were flying.

Well, not flying, exactly. But *teleporting*. I vaguely

recalled the first time he'd done that to me. I'd been so out of it that I hadn't really understood the sensations.

But I felt them now.

The whirlwind of energy whipping around me.

The tunnel-like sound of air in my ears.

The dizzying feeling of surpassing space and time.

My body was not meant for this sort of transport. Something my stomach told me as it churned violently inside me.

Fortunately, the journey ended almost as quickly as it'd begun. My back hit something smooth, my mind slowly registering that he'd set me in his car as the door closed beside me.

Then he was there, buckling me in as he took the driver's side.

The engine roared to life.

And we left in a blink, speeding out of the gates and down the road I'd been desperate to find when this test had begun.

My mind spun with questions and accusations, my world turning inside out and upside down in an instant.

This was what I'd craved for months.

But now I wasn't sure I desired it anymore.

He just wanted to hurt me. To torture me. To fail me when it suited him, just to subject me to a lifetime of pain.

The moon chase.

Becoming a lycan's pet.

Then the breeding farm.

Fuck, I was going to be sick.

All my anger and despair from earlier came roaring back, making me dizzy with fury.

I loathed this vampire. I didn't understand why he'd chosen me as the object of his torment, but I would give anything to make it stop.

He'd returned for me from wherever the hell he'd gone. And I'd *pined* for him.

Which was probably exactly what he'd wanted.

Goddess, how could I have been so stupid? Vampires loved to play with their food.

And I'd fallen right into his trap.

"Your fury is intoxicating," he murmured, his hand resting on the stick thing between us. "It's been a long time since I witnessed such emotion in a human. I'm rather pleased it's coming from you."

I gaped at him. "So you want me to be angry? To show emotion? To break decorum so you have a reason to punish me?" To what point? Vampires could do whatever they wanted. Why did he need a reason?

"Oh, I don't intend to punish you, Lily. I intend to reward you."

"By what? Failing me again?" I couldn't help the sarcastic reply. It was so unlike me. It broke a thousand rules. But I was done caring. Done playing this game. Done being the perfect prospect.

What was the point in cooperating when my compliance only led to pain?

"I won't be grading you on emotional performance, little flower. If I did, the others would kill you."

"They're going to kill me anyway," I muttered.

"Yes," he agreed, his voice holding an emotion I couldn't define. Probably because I didn't bother trying. He'd likely be there to watch the hunt, just to enjoy my suffering.

We didn't speak again for the rest of the drive.

Which was fine by me.

I didn't want to talk to him or be anywhere near him.

A complete contradiction to the last eight months.

Goddess, I'm a failure in every way. Maybe I deserved this fate after all.

He parked his car outside the palace, the exterior just as grandiose as I remembered.

Soft light illuminated the siding and highlighted various palm trees throughout the exterior landscaping. Stone steps led up to the opulent doors and the bejeweled interior.

I followed Master Cedric in a daze, my feet moving without my brain processing the action.

He led me through the interior courtyard, alongside a lightly flowing fountain, and through another door. Then up a set of stairs. Down a wide hall. And into a sitting room I recognized.

His quarters.

A human waited for us inside in a bowed position that made him sigh. "I didn't request blood. Just food. You may go."

The female shuddered and moved to stand, only to stumble part of the way. He blurred before me as he caught her by the elbow and helped her to her feet.

She swayed, her face paling as she mumbled an unintelligible sentence that sort of sounded like an apology.

"It's fine," he replied, his tone clipped. But his touch remained gentle in nature as he helped her move toward the door. "Take a moment to sit in the hallway and stretch your legs. If Mistress Adrienne questions you, tell her I commanded it."

"Yes, Sire," she whispered.

"Lily," he said from the doorway. "Grab the water from the table." He jerked his head toward the seating area, where a tray of food was waiting on the coffee table.

I did as he asked and brought it to him, my body still moving without my mind processing the actions.

He took it and handed it to the girl. "Drink this between stretches. Don't go back to Mistress Adrienne until you feel better. Understand?"

"Yes, Sire."

"Good." He guided her into the hallway and disappeared from view. He murmured something else to her that I didn't quite catch before returning and shutting the door.

It seemed quite odd to be so caring of a human. Maybe this one meant something to him. Or perhaps she was another player in his games.

"Go sit, Lily. You need to eat. Then we'll deal with the sand." He pointed at the couch and then to the tray of food before disappearing into his bedroom.

I frowned but did as he demanded.

Chicken. Green beans. Rice. Strawberries. My mouth salivated over that last item, my finger automatically grabbing it first. But Master Cedric appeared out of thin air, taking it from me and putting it back in the bowl.

"Eat your other food first." He set a bottle of water down to replace the one he'd given to the human. "I'll handle the strawberries."

My mouth tightened, my taste buds not in the mood to engage in whatever cruel game he intended to begin. I just wanted to eat the berries. They were sweet and unlike anything else the university fed me.

But I didn't want him to see my disappointment.

So I stuffed a green bean into my mouth instead.

Then I used the water to swallow it down.

Master Cedric sat beside me, his thigh brushing mine as he picked up a knife. My heart skipped a beat, my skin breaking out in goose bumps.

Except he didn't bring the blade anywhere near me.

Instead, he started removing the strawberry stems.

I ate my chicken while he worked, my gaze glued to his athletic hands and the long fingers wielding the knife. Each slice was precise, the strawberries remaining mostly whole as he removed the green part.

My green beans and chicken were gone by the time he finished, only the rice left. I nibbled my lip, my stomach feeling rather full already from the larger-than-usual meal.

"Do you want the rice?" he asked softly.

"I… I want the strawberries more," I admitted.

He nodded and handed me the bowl. "You'll enjoy them more this time."

I'd liked them just fine last time, but I didn't tell him that. Instead, I popped one of the berries into my mouth and nearly groaned at the sweetness of the fruit.

Sweet yet tart.

Juicy.

Perfect.

He was right—I did like them more this time. He said nothing as I devoured the bowl, his dark eyes on me the whole time. I couldn't even be bothered by his intrigue; my mouth was too pleased to let anything taint the moment.

When I finished, he stood with the tray and took it to the hallway. I heard him speaking again and assumed it was to the servant.

Her soft response confirmed it.

He gave a nod and returned to the room, then held out his hand for me. "Stand up and follow me. We need to wash the sand out of your hair."

My insides flipped over at what that meant—*another bath.*

Except he walked right past the tub when we entered his bathroom.

And went to the giant walk-in shower instead.

Three showerheads came on at once, the rainfall effect

rather hypnotic. I watched the droplets flow for a beat, my mind oddly at ease.

Until Master Cedric interrupted my view.

His eyes reminded me of a thunderstorm, all dark and ominous. Yet his touch was deceptively gentle as he brushed his knuckles across my cheek. "Take off your clothes, Lily."

I almost reminded him that my name wasn't Lily anymore, but it felt pointless to say. He enjoyed tormenting me and would probably reply with something to give me hope just so he could rip it away again later.

Sighing, I bent to remove my shoes. Then I slid off my athletic pants and stood upright to remove my shirt, leaving me naked before him.

Lightning flashed in his gaze as he surveyed my nude state.

I half expected him to try to eat me.

However, he surprised me by unbuttoning his dress shirt and laying it over a marble counter. He placed his shoes and socks beside mine. Then he unfastened his belt and pulled off his trousers before folding them both over his shirt.

His body was a work of art, all athletic, lean lines that flexed and moved in a manner that hypnotized me more than the showerheads had.

Then his thumbs hooked into the thin fabric hiding his groin and began to inch it down.

My mouth went dry.

He hadn't done this the last time we'd been in here. He'd kept that small barrier between us.

But not anymore.

Now it was dragging down his strong thighs and long, muscular legs.

I swallowed.

Master Cedric was already hard to admire in a clothed state. Naked? He was like a god demanding to be worshipped.

My knees wobbled with the need to bend, to kneel, to pray for his touch.

I couldn't stop staring.

I couldn't stop studying.

I couldn't stop *craving*.

This was the worst kind of trick. Vampires were alluring by nature. It was how they subdued their prey. Even knowing that, I was a slave to my urges.

His stomach flexed as he added his boxers to his clothing pile, his arms bulging with power and tangible strength. I tried to focus on that perfection, to not follow the light dusting of hair from his navel downward, but my innate desire to *see* him coerced my gaze into dropping.

Long. Proud. Hard.

Oh, Goddess.

I swallowed again for an entirely different reason. My throat courses had prepared me for a male of his size. But I suddenly wondered if I'd been prepared enough.

He reached for me, his fingers grasping my chin to tug my gaze upward. "Looking at me like that is going to lead to activities we're not ready for yet." His fingers danced along my jaw, then down my neck, before grazing my nipple in a light caress that made my toes curl on his way to grabbing my hand.

That touch might not have been on purpose, but it certainly felt intentional. And the underlying amusement in his dark irises confirmed that suspicion.

He tugged me toward the shower, leading me inside, and directly under the rainfall.

I closed my eyes.

His hand left mine, his fingertips trailing up my arm to

my shoulder and into my hair to brush the dampening strands.

"I missed you, Lily," he whispered, his breath a kiss against my cheek as his opposite hand went to my hip. "This shower is for you. You make the rules. You tell me what you need, what you want. And I'll give it to you, Lily, no matter the ask."

LILY

Master Cedric's lips lightly touched mine, sending a shiver through my being.

This was another trick. A game I didn't know how to play. Yet his words lulled me into a soothing state, my entire being shuddering beneath the sudden change from tensed to relaxed.

It was as though he'd enchanted me with a few softly spoken statements.

I knew better than to accept them.

But some broken part of me wanted them to be real. To believe him. To *trust* him.

An insane notion.

A lethal one.

Yet I had nothing to lose. He'd already outlined my fate. Why not indulge and take advantage of this small offering? Perhaps it would be enough to fill my dreams at night.

Or maybe it would become the worst kind of torture.

A beautiful torment to haunt my dark future.

Was it worth the risk?

Should I ignore the offer?

Did he even mean it?

Maybe this was all just a way to use my yearnings against me. Should I give him that playing hand?

"Tell me what you want, Lily," he whispered against my mouth, his fingers still combing through my hair. "Tell me how to make this up to you."

I frowned. His words sounded almost apologetic. But why? Because he felt bad for telling me about the moon chase?

It hadn't been the news I'd desired to hear.

However, I preferred to know the truth, even though it hurt.

Just like I wanted his truth now. "Why are you doing this to me?" I asked, my voice a rasp of sound beneath the streaming water. "Why did you choose me for this game?"

I wanted to at least understand that part. Not that I could change it. Not that it would help me in the future. But I had to know.

"Why do you enjoy torturing me?" I whispered. "Was it a mistake I made? Something I said? Because of my inferior fighting skills?" Now that I had started speaking, I couldn't seem to stop. "Is that why you torment me? Or is it because I asked for help?"

I stilled as that question left my lips.

"That's it, isn't it? This is all because I broke decorum and asked for guidance." The words were more for me than for him, my mind finally understanding where I'd gone wrong.

Of course it was that error in judgment.

I knew better than to question a Master.

Yet I'd done it anyway.

And now I was paying for the mistake.

"That's why I'm going to the moon chase," I breathed. "A punishment for questioning your authority.

When all I wanted was to understand why you kept failing me."

I felt numb. Cold. Frozen in place.

"I'd ask you to kill me, but you won't." The words were barely audible. "You want me to suffer. You enjoy it." A tear escaped the edge of my closed eye. "I hate you, Master Cedric. I hate that you've done this to me. And I hate that, despite it all, I still crave more."

My heart shattered in my chest, a fragile part of me breaking beneath the weight of these revelations.

All I wanted was to curl into a ball.

And die.

But he wouldn't allow it.

He'd force me to feel. Play with me until he grew bored. And leave me to my fate.

"Just do whatever you want," I said, my voice brittle. "I won't fight you. I won't even question you. This shower isn't for me; it's for you. So let's skip the part where you inspire false hope, and go straight to what you truly want."

I opened my eyes to meet his tumultuous gaze.

"Do you want to test me again? My oral skills have improved. Shall I show you?" My voice sounded dead to my ears. But maybe that was what he wanted—*a dried-up flower.*

His expression gave nothing away, his dark eyes dancing over my features as his grip tightened against my hip. "Do you want to know why I kept failing you?" His voice held an edge to it that reminded me of jagged ice.

"Does it matter?" I countered. "You'll fail me regardless of how I perform. I could be perfect and you'll still fail me."

"You *are* perfect," he bit back. "That's why I kept failing you, Lily. To urge you down a different path. Because I saw where this one was heading. Yet you defied me and kept pushing, and now you're going to the moon chase, where the lycans are going to fucking rip you apart. Do you think that pleases me?"

"Yes," I answered without even needing to think it through. "You've been torturing me since the beginning. You'll enjoy watching the end, too."

He snorted. "You've misunderstood everything I've given you."

My eyebrows rose. "And what have you given me, Master Cedric? A name that you took away? A glimmer of hope that you also took away? Negative feedback about my fighting abilities? A negative grade for sexual skills you didn't even give me a real opportunity to perform?"

My breath came out in a pant, heat rising to my cheeks as my heart thundered in my chest.

"Or are you talking about your blood?" I continued. "Blood you used to heal me so you could break me again, right?"

His fingers fisted my hair, his grip bruising my hip. "Do you know where sexually skilled humans with fighting spirits go after Blood Day?"

"Moon chase," I hissed, aware of that knowledge because he'd blatantly spelled it out for me.

"So why do you think I failed you in both of those areas, Lily?" His gaze darkened. "To deter you from heading down that path. Yet you ran headfirst for it the moment I left. And why? To prove me wrong?"

"To see you again," I bit back. "I wanted a chance to show you that you were wrong about me. But you weren't there. So I took the next class and the next, hoping for the opportunity to demonstrate my improvements." Because I was a sad, pathetic human with an idiotic infatuation with a Master.

He glowered. "You want to demonstrate your

improvements now? Let me fuck you in the ass against that shower wall, just to see if you can take a vampire cock the same way you could a human one?"

"If that's what it takes, then yes," I snapped, entirely lost and confused as to how the conversation had come to this point. I couldn't even remember what he'd said to make me start talking. But I was so angry at him for failing me. For driving me to such extremes just to prove him wrong.

"You're a stubborn little brat," he muttered, shaking his head. "I failed you because I wanted to make your inevitable death as peaceful as possible. You don't meet the physical requirements for a Vigil. You're not marked as eligible for the Immortal Cup. And you were on the fast track for going to a harem. So I tried to push you down a different path toward servitude instead, hoping you would end up somewhere less violent. But now you're a prime moon chase candidate."

He released me so suddenly that I almost fell.

"I didn't check your records while I was gone because there wasn't a damn thing I could do to help you." He faced the wall and slammed his palms against the tiles so hard that I jumped. "And now there's little I can do to fix this."

I gaped at his back, all of his statements slamming into me with the ferocity of a stun gun.

"I could kill you," he continued, his fingers curling against the marble wall. "I *should* kill you. That would be the kind solution."

He faced me once more, his expression sending a chill down my spine as he reached for me again. I took a step backward on instinct, but his palm curled around my nape and pulled me forward.

"But I can't," he whispered, his gaze falling to my

mouth. "I can't kill you, Lily. The very notion of it sends me into a blind rage. You've become my obsession. Everything I've done these last few months has been in an effort to return to you before Blood Day. To see you one last time. To touch you." He shook his head. "I don't want to hurt you, Lily. I want to give you life. To make you bloom. Provide you with enough memories to last an eternity."

I stopped breathing, the intensity in his words and expression rendering me speechless.

This was all likely another manipulation, a way to break me irrevocably.

But it felt so incredibly real.

"I'm too selfish to kill you, Lily." He walked me backward until my shoulder blades hit the wall. Then he pinned me there with his hips as his hands cupped my cheeks. "Ask me for anything else, and it's yours. But please don't ask me for death."

CEDRIC

A DARK LAUGH ECHOED THROUGH MY THOUGHTS AS I
repeated my confession in my mind.

Death had been my purpose for millennia.

Yet it was the one thing I couldn't give to Lily.

A better man would put her out of her misery. But I
wasn't a good man. I wanted Lily, even if just for a
month.

She'd die.

I'd live.

And the memories of our time together would follow
me for eternity, or until I found a new flower.

Hmm. I ran my thumbs along the hollows beneath her
pretty eyes. *No. There will never be another Lily.*

I'd lived several thousands of years and had never
found a female like her. She captivated me in a bewitching
way, making me wonder if some higher being had sent her
here just to torture me.

She'd accused me of tormenting her.

And maybe I had to an extent.

Just not for the reasons she'd described.

Lily's lips brushed mine, her eyes holding a myriad of

questions that she couldn't seem to voice. So she responded with her mouth, kissing me for the first time.

Oh, she'd returned my embraces with passion in the past.

But this was the first time she'd taken a kiss for herself.

The first time she'd demonstrated an interest that went beyond her regular training.

I let her lead, my lips responding to hers with the same gentle stroke. I'd told her this shower was for her, and I'd meant it. This was my version of an apology, a way to start over and create our own beginning.

All my cards were on the table.

All my truths.

Whatever she wanted, I'd give her. *Except for death.* That I would never bestow upon her. But I would kill for her if she asked me to.

This obsession was borderline toxic, the lengths I would go to for her edging on suicidal.

I'd dreamt of stealing her before Blood Day.

I'd dreamt of claiming she'd died, then keeping her for myself.

I'd dreamt of running away with her.

But they were all fantasies that could never come to fruition.

Silvano would find me. Then he'd take out his anger on her rather than me, while forcing me to watch. And I could never subject her to that fate.

Lily pulled back, her pretty irises more blue than green now. "I don't understand you."

My lips curled at her admission. "How about we play a game?" I suggested, my hands sliding from her cheeks to her neck. "You can ask me whatever you want while I wash your hair. And I'll answer every question."

Her expression had immediately turned wary at my

mention of a *game*—a term I belatedly realized wasn't the best to use in this situation. And that wariness had quickly melted into suspicion after my explanation.

Her gaze narrowed as she asked, "In exchange for what?"

"I get to touch you." I shrugged. "That's all I want." I reached up to tug on a strand of her hair. "I won't even make it sexual. I'll just take care of you while you ask me questions."

Because this was for her.

I would merely benefit from having her here.

She swallowed, her expression telling me that she didn't believe me at all. But her training kicked in as she nodded. "Okay."

Part of me wanted to push for a stronger acceptance. However, it would be more prudent to prove her wrong.

So I would.

I pressed a kiss to her forehead and stepped back beneath the water. "Stand over here," I instructed, showing her with a gesture where I wanted her. Then I went to the corner shelf of the shower to find some supplies.

She did as I asked, her bottom lip catching between her teeth as she observed me.

I stayed quiet, allowing her to think as I returned to set the bottles on the floor beside her. When she didn't speak, I busied myself by running my fingers through her hair once more and ensuring her strands were damp enough.

It wasn't until I gently pushed her a step forward that she finally asked, "You left the university?"

A safe question, I mused. *Since I've already insinuated that.*

"Yes." I didn't elaborate because I wanted her to pry, to step outside of her zone and ask me what she truly wanted to know.

I bent to pick up a bottle and poured some shampoo into my hand.

"Where did you go?" she whispered.

"To Silvano Region." I started massaging the shampoo into her hair. "And also Clemente Clan."

"L-lycans?"

"Yes."

"Is that where I'll go?"

I frowned at her question. "I don't know. Your records don't show a definitive location yet." But I hoped she didn't end up there. Alpha Walter was a narcissistic prick with a power complex.

Hence the reason I'd been called home.

"So you weren't there about the moon chase?" she asked as I pulled her back beneath the water to rinse the shampoo from her hair.

"Why would I go there for…?" I trailed off, my brow furrowing as I spun her to face me. "You think I went there to make arrangements to watch you be raped and killed?" I couldn't hold back the fury in my tone. Because *what the fuck*? "Why the fuck would I want to watch that?"

Her eyes widened.

Then she flinched as soap entered her gaze.

I cursed and helped her rinse the shampoo from her face, chastising myself for handling her so roughly. She might have had my blood in her, but that didn't make her invincible.

After carefully rinsing the shampoo from her hair, I gently pulled her out from under the water again.

"Silvano called me back for a favor. He needed me to remind Alpha Walter of a few key items. Which is a polite way to say that I had to beat the shit out of a few of his wolves. And it took several long months for the message to be properly delivered."

207

I shouldn't be telling her any of this.

Hell, I shouldn't have even divulged what I truly wanted from her.

But it felt good to be truthful.

It felt right to be honest with her about my intentions, too.

She didn't trust me because I hadn't given her any reason to put her faith in me. However, now she was mine for a month.

Silvano had promised me two years without interference so long as I helped him with his wolf problem.

I'd taken the offer.

For Lily.

For this single month where I could coexist with her without any other responsibilities.

Of course, I hadn't factored Prince Khalid into my plans.

But I'd feel him out over breakfast and determine if he would be a problem then.

"It goes without saying that anything I share with you is another secret between us," I said softly, my palm cupping her jaw. "What I did for Silvano can't be shared. And it had nothing to do with a moon chase."

She swallowed, her head bobbing a little. "They share a border, right?"

"Yes. And they've been working together. But Walter is a cocky son of a bitch. So Silvano asked me to remind him of his place." More like *commanded* me. But I'd been able to negotiate my two-year reprieve as payment.

However, at the end, I would officially become his sovereign.

"By beating up his wolves," she whispered.

"I have a knack for violence," I replied, bending to pick up another bottle—this one conditioner. "I'm also very good at sneaking into places undetected." Such as clan territory. Walter's enforcers didn't stand a chance.

"That sounds dangerous."

I shrugged and started lathering her hair again. "It's the nature of my existence."

Although, I usually entered situations like that without fearing death. This time had been a bit different because Lily had given me something to look forward to. Something to live for.

"I've always been drawn to violence and righting wrongs. I even made a living off of it for a very long time. But when the world changed, I shifted into an enforcer-like role for Silvano."

Enforcer wasn't the official term, but it was one she would understand from her lycan politics class.

"He calls me when he needs me," I clarified lamely. "However, he's just given me two more years before I have to join him in the political arena."

"As his sovereign," she whispered as I guided her beneath the spray again.

"As his sovereign," I echoed. "It's not a future I desire, but it's the one I'm required to accept."

Silence fell between us as I finished cleaning her hair.

Then I moved on to her body, using the soap and sponge I'd picked up from the corner.

"What future do you desire?" she asked after several minutes of quiet.

I knelt to start with her legs as I considered her question. *Peace* seemed too vague a response. "I'm honestly not sure anymore," I finally settled on. "This new world is too different from the old one for me to give you a good answer."

"What do you mean by 'new world'?" she asked, her

expression no longer exuding that earlier wariness or suspicion. Just a healthy dose of curiosity.

I ran the sponge up her thighs while holding her gaze. "The world wasn't always like this. There was a time when humans ruled and my kind lived among them in secret. But then lycans were discovered, and the human governments responded by trying to weaponize them. It didn't end well for the mortals."

An understatement.

Nearly ninety percent of humankind was killed for the atrocity. The remaining ten percent were enslaved.

And the Blood Alliance was formed between the vampire royals and lycan alphas.

"It's not a history the universities teach humans. All they want you to know is that we are in charge. To suggest otherwise is dangerous and could lead to a revolution." A laughable suggestion, really.

The only way a revolution could be successful was with vampires and lycans at the helm.

I gently turned Lily to begin soaping the back of her legs while I let her process everything I'd just revealed. She shivered as I neared her ass, her skin prickling with goose bumps as the air around us seemed to shift.

I inhaled, smiling as I scented her sweet arousal. It'd been there the whole time, just subtle and slightly subdued because of our conversation.

It would be so easy to seduce her. Just slip the sponge between her spread thighs and brush her pretty pink flesh.

I swallowed and forced the desire away, reminding myself that this was about her.

She was in charge.

I would follow her lead.

And if she happened to turn around and guide my face to her sweet pussy, I would happily oblige.

Alas, she remained still.

So I focused on thoroughly soaping up her beautiful, firm ass before standing to work on her back.

She continued to tremble yet remained silent.

I'd given her a lot to consider. If she wanted to ask more questions later, I'd allow it.

I rotated her again to work on her torso, my sponge expertly creating suds against her breasts and abdomen before venturing to her arms.

All the while, she watched me from beneath hooded eyes.

I ended our intimate moment with a quick stroke of the sponge against her shaved mound and added a swift caress between her thighs, then set aside my supplies on the ground and rinsed her a final time.

When I finished, I met her gaze and said, "Game over. But we can play another one, if you want to."

Again, maybe not the best choice of words. However, I wanted her to fully grasp my version of a game. Maybe that would help her understand me better.

Rather than wait for her to reply, I took a step back.

"I'm going to put my hands on the wall. If you want to touch me, you can. The soap is right there." I gestured to where I'd set it against the marble floor. "If you don't want to play, then step out of the shower and take one of the towels. I'll wash up and join you when I'm done."

With that blatant offer, I turned and pressed my palms to the stone-tile wall.

And waited.

Hoping she would understand the purpose behind my offer. *An apology.* Not direct. Not obvious. Just a subtle way of submitting to her needs.

My version of displaying intent.

Proving to her that I wanted her to choose me, not bow because of her training.

I would understand if she stepped out—I absolutely deserved that reaction.

I just hoped she wouldn't.

I closed my eyes.

What's it going to be, little flower? I wondered. *Are you ready for my version of a game? Or are you going to run and hide?*

LILY

I stared at Master Cedric's back, indulging in the undisturbed view of his flawless form.

He was gorgeous.

Tall. Athletically lean. Broad shoulders. Tapered waist. Sculpted backside. Long, muscular legs.

An enforcer.

I understood that term in the lycan sense. But what did it mean for a vampire?

He certainly looked lethal. However, that was rather standard for his kind.

Yet he'd taken on a rather unimposing position against the wall.

For me.

My head spun with all his comments and actions. I hadn't expected him to really answer my questions, but he had. And with more information than I'd ever anticipated.

He'd been gone this whole time.

He'd tried to help me.

He doesn't want me to go to the moon chase or a harem.

"Did you give me the water?" I asked, the curiosity one that tumbled from my lips before I could stop it.

He'd already said our previous game was over.

But I'd been so overwhelmed by all his responses that I hadn't thought of this question until now.

Until I'd realized how wrongly I'd understood this situation. *Because he's been helping me in his own way. Not hurting me.*

"Yes," he replied without looking at me. "I couldn't leave a note without risking your safety. So I left you nutrients instead."

"What would your note have said?" I wondered aloud. "If you could have left one."

"That you were my Lily and I would be back for you." He uttered the words without hesitation, telling me he'd thought about it before I'd asked. Which meant it was true.

"You took away my name."

"To protect you, yes." He still didn't turn around or look at me, his palms steady against the stone tile. "You can't be Lily at the university. Only here where you're alone with me."

That's why he reminded me not to scream the last time he bit me, I realized. *He was protecting me.*

The sudden understanding of his actions had me feeling dizzy. There was so much I hadn't interpreted correctly. And now I had a thousand new questions regarding his intent.

But I couldn't voice them.

I was still too busy processing everything else.

Master Cedric failed me to keep me from going to the moon chase or a harem.

Master Cedric gave me the water. He didn't actually take away my name. He came back for me.

Everything spun around me, the water sounding distant to my ears. It was too much to process at once. Too much to accept. Too much *hope.*

Master Cedric caught me as my knees buckled, his arms coming around me as he lifted me into the air. "That's not how this game is played, Lily," he murmured, his eyes a pulsating darkness that only made me dizzier.

He moved to sit on the marble bench decorating one side of the shower, his strong body easily holding mine as he settled me onto his lap.

"Just breathe," he whispered as my head fell against his shoulder. "Inhale and exhale and try to relax."

His hypnotic tone washed over me, warming my insides. He pressed his lips to my head, his strength swathing me in a cocoon of protection.

The adrenaline and horror of the evening all seemed to be catching up to me. My body ached in a strange way. I wasn't sore so much as exhausted. Mentally. Physically. *Emotionally*.

I'd been lost one minute and floored the next.

Master Cedric's comments about the former world still circulated in the back of my mind.

Humans used to rule, I marveled. *Lycans and vampires hid.*

What a strange concept.

What would that world even be like?

I couldn't picture it at all. It made no sense. Why would the superior beings hide?

Master Cedric kissed my temple, his palm rubbing my arm as he held me close. It was such a strange sensation to be held like this, especially by a being as powerful as him.

Vampires and lycans never exuded care or affection. Sensuality and hunger, yes. But nothing like this.

I struggled to correlate this version of Master Cedric to the one who used to lead my fighting courses. To the one who had failed me without remorse.

It was like his time away had changed him.

Yet he'd been just as hard on me earlier during the

course exercise. So perhaps not. Perhaps I was just seeing a new layer of his personality.

He'd carried me after I'd been beaten in his class. He'd cured me, too.

Maybe it really was him after all.

Or maybe this was just another manipulation meant to break me.

I sighed, tired from all the thinking and processing of details. I just wanted to exist for a moment without too much thought. To escape to an oblivion where I could merely feel without worrying about anything else.

He'd offered me that escape in the form of a game.

"I want to play," I whispered, my head rotating back to survey his stunning features. "I want to play your new game."

Master Cedric's thighs tensed beneath me as his lips curled. "All right."

He didn't immediately move, his dark gaze holding mine for a long moment. His irises gave nothing away, his expression unreadable apart from the small grin flirting with his mouth.

That slight smile made him even more handsome, almost cruelly so. His jawline and cheekbones were flawless and symmetrical, and his eyes were dusted with long black lashes.

So beautiful.

And he'd given me permission to touch him. To explore him. To bathe him like he had me.

I want that, I thought, my blood heating with the notion. *I want to touch him.*

My courses had prepared me for it.

But Six was nothing like Master Cedric—a fact that didn't intimidate me so much as excite me.

I should be afraid.

I should be running away in search of a towel.

However, I couldn't move. I wanted to play his game.

"Now you're ready to play," he whispered, lifting me off of him and setting me on my feet.

I nearly swayed, more from the loss of contact than my previous dizziness, but his hands caught my hips as he stood behind me. Then he slowly maneuvered me beneath the showerheads again.

"The sponge is there," he said against my ear as he pointed at the item in question. "The soaps are here." His hand moved to gesture at the bottles. "I'll be right over there." He indicated the wall he'd been against minutes ago. "The game ends when you leave the shower."

He pressed a kiss to my temple and released me.

Then he stepped over to the marble slab and placed his palms against the wall once more.

I swallowed, my gaze running over his flawless physique to his muscular ass. *I get to touch that.*

My insides warmed at the thought, my hands already moving toward the sponge. It wasn't like the ones I used in my service classes. This was soft and gauzy rather than tough and firm.

Master Cedric had gently created suds with this. No harsh or strenuous scrubbing, just tender, coaxing brushes against my skin.

I would do my best to mimic those movements.

I applied some soap, the minty fragrance reminding me of Master Cedric, and slowly made my way toward him.

He didn't move, his body relaxed in this pose as he waited for me to touch him.

I considered where to start, every part of him calling to me at once.

His ass probably the most. So I would save that for last as a treat.

I knelt to begin on his ankles and calves. *So firm*, I marveled. *Lightly dusted with hair, too.*

The university required frequent shaving of lower limbs and other areas. At least for the females. Some males were required to trim as well. Although, the rules seemed to vary for men. I never paid much attention, my focus on my own requirements instead.

However, I rather liked Master Cedric's legs. They were masculine and strong and led to sinful parts of him I longed to explore.

He'd failed me on my sexual performance. I understood now that he'd done it to steer me away from that path, but that didn't dissuade my need to prove him wrong.

I'd studied hard over these last eight months, longing for an opportunity to prove myself to him. To show him I was worth a second chance.

It'd been my obsession.

And now I was on my knees behind him, gently creating soapsuds against his skin. His thighs flexed beneath my touch, his limbs seeming to tighten as I slipped my hands between his legs to soap up the front. I didn't touch his groin, just his quads and back down to his knees and then his shins.

I didn't stop until every inch of his legs was soapy. Then I stood. "Do you want to rinse off your lower half? Or should I continue?" I asked, my voice throatier than before.

"You're in charge, Lily. Tell me your preference."

I swallowed. "I... I think you should wash off while I get more soap." I'd used most of it on his legs and needed more.

His palms lowered and he turned, his erection nudging

my stomach. I bit back a yelp in response, my cheeks heating at the strong evidence of his desire.

He cupped my face with one hand and pressed a kiss to my lips. "You're doing very well, little flower. Don't run away now."

My throat worked, my eyes widening a little. "I don't want to run away." It came out in a whisper, the words oddly choked.

"Good," he replied, kissing me again. "I'm going to go rinse my thoroughly soaped-up legs." He sounded amused, his dark eyes glittering.

I froze as he moved around me.

Then I turned as though he held me by a string, my focus going to his front and the evidence of his arousal. He'd been hard for most of our shower. I'd even felt his thickness beneath me when he'd held me on his lap. But it hadn't registered until now that I could indulge in that part of him.

He said I was in charge.

And he was hard.

That meant I could please him—that I was *already* pleasing him. Maybe that was the point of the game.

He said the game would end when I left the shower.

But what if I made him come? Would the game end there?

"Soap, Lily," he murmured without looking at me. He had his head tipped back beneath the water, his fingers combing through his damp, dark strands.

His abdomen rippled with the motion, his muscles beckoning me forward in a silent invitation to touch him.

I dropped the sponge, my fingers needing to be free for this experience.

His hands went still in his hair as my palm met his abdomen. *Solid. Hard. Male.*

Six didn't feel like this. He wasn't soft, but he wasn't Master Cedric.

Goddess, *no one* was Master Cedric.

He redefined beauty, captivating me in a way none of my previous Masters ever had. I wanted to memorize every inch of him with my fingers and tongue.

Cleaning him no longer applied.

I wanted something different.

Something sinful.

Something I shouldn't crave but refused to ignore.

His approval.

His pleasure.

His groans.

My lips went to his pec, the kiss tentative as I glanced up to read his expression. He'd opened his eyes, the dark rings around his pupils fathomless.

His arms were flexed from keeping his hands in his hair.

He appeared to be waiting to see what I would do next.

I was waiting to see what I would do next.

I licked my lips, the motion grazing his chest as well. The watery droplets on his skin were refreshing, making me desire another taste.

So I indulged in the need, parting my lips to place an open-mouthed kiss over his nipple.

Then I started a familiar path down—not because I'd done this on him, but because I'd been trained on what trail to follow. It quickly turned new and exciting, his abdomen a landscape of concaves and tense lines.

I loved it.

Each divot represented an erotic experience, my mouth hungry to navigate and learn every part of him.

When I found the dusting of hair that led down from his belly button, I nearly groaned.

My thighs clenched, warmth flooding through my veins at the notion of intimately exploring him with my tongue.

I fluidly went to my knees, my legs bending in a practiced way while my core strength engaged to keep me steady. The trick was not to touch the male when kneeling, something Master Peyton said the superior species expected of their human servants.

We were only supposed to touch vampires and lycans in an arousing manner, not in any manner meant to aid our efforts. And that included using a Master for balance.

Alas, my fingers protested my movement because I *wanted* to touch him. To grab his hips and move to his firm backside. To squeeze and revel in the athleticism of his form.

He was so perfect. So handsome. So *big*.

I nearly gulped as his manhood came within inches of my mouth. The head was wide, but not unmanageable. I could easily wrap my lips around it and swallow.

However, his length gave me pause.

I'd felt it against my lower belly, but seeing it up close provided significantly more detail.

It's a good thing I took throat training, I thought, my mouth suddenly dry. *What if it's not enough?*

"Are you planning to wash me with your mouth?" Master Cedric asked, his tone holding a touch of irritation in it that caused my eyes to return to his.

Tumultuous irises stared down at me, the look rivaling his voice.

I'm taking too long to perform, I realized, my heart skipping a beat.

Humans weren't supposed to question their superiors. They just took whatever was given to them.

Including accepting a large cock down the throat.

I knew better than to pause and evaluate his size.

This was about his pleasure, something he clearly craved.

And I intended to prove to him that I could properly please him.

"Sorry, Master Cedric," I whispered as I wrapped my hand around the base of him. "Your impressive size took me by surprise." I hoped the compliment would defuse the situation.

However, his thunderous expression told me it hadn't.

I pressed my lips to his bulbous head, hoping to make him forget my infraction.

Except I found my hair wrapped around his fist in the next second.

I opened my mouth, expecting him to drive himself down my throat in anger.

But he pulled me away instead, his own knees bending as he joined me on the floor. "*This* is not the game we're playing, Lily. I don't want your mouth on my cock. I want your hands on my body. Exploring. Touching. *Learning*. And I certainly don't want you sucking me off according to university standards."

Ice drizzled through my veins, chasing away the warmth.

He… he doesn't want me to please him?

"Is this because I failed before?" I asked, confused, as I thought he'd said I hadn't actually failed. But maybe I'd misunderstood. "I've been training. I can do better. I know I paused, but—"

He yanked on my hair, the action making me wince. "This shower is for you, Lily. Not for me." His grip lessened then, his gaze falling to my mouth before meeting my eyes once more. "When I fuck your mouth, it will be because you actually want me to, not because you think it's what I desire."

"But isn't it what you want?" I asked, my hand finding his hardness once more. "You're aroused."

"Of course I'm aroused, Lily. I'm naked in a shower with you."

"Then let me please you," I whispered. "I... I *want* to please you." I did. And not just because of the failure before, but because I'd dreamt of it for months. "I want to taste you. I want to see your pleasure."

Some of the anger left his expression, his eyes searching mine. "I almost believe you."

"Because it's true," I told him.

"This is your training talking."

I shook my head, then nodded a little because he wasn't wrong, but he wasn't right either. "I'm trained, yes. But I trained for you. I want a chance to show you what I know and what I can do. You said I didn't really fail. But I want to know what it's like to pass. To meet your expectations. To please *you*."

I realized it sounded naïve and borderline obsessive. But it was the truth.

"You said this game ends when I leave the shower, but I'm still here," I continued. "And I want to prove to you that I can win. That I can impress you. Please, Master Cedric. Will you let me pleasure you?"

CEDRIC

"No." Not because I didn't want it, but because this wasn't how I wanted her to beg.

Lily was desperate to prove her worth to me without understanding that she already had. That was why I'd returned for her, why I'd brought her back here.

I already wanted her.

She had more than passed every test imaginable.

But her expression fell now at my refusal, her shoulders bowing in a defeat similar to the one I'd witnessed months ago before I'd left.

I released her hair to grasp her chin and pulled her gaze back to mine. "You're not ready to please me yet," I informed her gently. "But you will be soon."

Because I intended to teach her my ways, to show her what true rapture meant.

We'd only begun our journey together months ago.

Tonight, I would take us another step forward.

Sadness filled her gaze as she released my throbbing cock. "Yes, Master Cedric." Her voice held a note of despair to it that made me sigh. *This* was why she couldn't properly please me yet. She'd been indoctrinated in this world of savagery, her mind warped to a point of no return.

I'd have to break some of that conditioning to make her fully understand.

Perhaps it was cruel to do this to her mere weeks before her Blood Day, yet it was the only real gift I could provide for her—memories to warm her heart and mind on her journey to death.

"I'm not failing you, Lily," I promised her. "And I'm not doubting your skills or training. I know what courses you've taken, but those classes were not designed with my preferences in mind."

Such as willing submission, not forced submission.

"When you call me *Master* in the bedroom, it will be because I earned the title." It would be when she actually understood what it meant. And that kink might never even come to fruition between us, which was okay with me. I could handle all sorts of roles in the bedroom.

But I couldn't have her like this.

I didn't want a placid doll.

I wanted a blossoming flower. I wanted my Lily.

"I'm Cedric when we're alone. I know I took that back before, but I've explained my reasons for that. And now that you're mine for the next month, you can freely call me Cedric again."

Unless someone told me I couldn't have her.

However, the only one with the authority to do so was Prince Khalid. I doubted he would deny my request, but I'd find out during our evening breakfast.

Her blue-green eyes studied me. "I still don't understand you."

I smiled. "You will." *Or maybe she won't.*

It didn't matter.

What mattered was our time left together. "Our game

isn't finished, Lily. My legs are clean, but that's only the lower half of me."

Her nostrils flared, her expression coming alive with renewed interest. "I… I can still touch you?"

"Yes. But I don't want you on your knees tonight." I stood and pulled her up with me by grasping her shoulders. "Now grab the sponge and finish the game."

I took a step back to see what she would do.

Her eyes ran over me, her pupils pulsating as she took in my still-hard shaft.

She swallowed, her cheeks reddening.

Then she went for the soap, forgoing the sponge.

I arched a brow, curious as to what she intended.

She squirted a healthy amount of body wash into her palm, set the bottle down, and rubbed her hands together. "I want to touch you without the sponge."

My lips curled at her attempt to be in charge. Unfortunately, her tone made it sound more like a question than a statement.

However, it was a good start to her showing some sexual independence.

So I provided the confirmation she needed to continue. "Proceed."

Her shoulders fell, some of the tension seeming to leave her as she approached me.

I kept my arms loose at my sides, my focus on reading her facial cues. Determination etched a stern line into her forehead, her lips pursed and her gaze intent.

I half expected her to grab my dick and demand that I let her prove her worth.

But she pressed her palms to my abdomen instead, her touch warm as she began to lather the soap against my skin. She carefully cleansed below my belly button before venturing higher along my rib cage and up to my chest.

She was precise and methodical, ensuring that not an inch of the front of my torso was untouched—except for the area leading to my groin. "Rinse," she said as she went back for more soap.

I almost told her to go down and finish the front but decided to obey instead. Perhaps she didn't trust herself to touch me there again.

Or maybe she thought she wasn't allowed after I'd denied her request to suck me off.

I'd wait to see what she did next before I commented.

Once I finished rinsing my front, she began on my back. Then she worked on my sides again, followed by my arms.

My ass and cock were both left untouched.

Either she was trying to tease me, or she didn't fully grasp the concept of this game. I didn't mind her exploring; I just didn't want her to focus on my pleasure.

She watched as I rinsed off once more, showing no signs of going for the soap again.

"Are you finished?" I finally asked when she didn't speak or move for a solid sixty seconds.

"I…" She swallowed, her brow coming down. "Am I allowed to…?"

"You'll have to finish that question before I can answer it," I replied.

She frowned, her gaze dropping to my groin. "You don't want me to please you."

"Oh, I very much want you to please me," I corrected her. "But this isn't about me, Lily. What do *you* want?"

"To please you," she said without missing a beat.

Of course she would say that. It was exactly the sort of statement her previous instructors would have told her to use.

"How about you start by finishing what you started

with the soap," I suggested instead. Because I knew she wanted to touch me. She just didn't understand how to voice that interest.

By the time we stepped out of this shower, she would better comprehend my expectations.

She studied me for a moment, then bent to grab the sponge. "I thought you preferred your hands?" I murmured, aware that I was taunting her. But she needed the subtle push.

Lily remained in her position for a beat, providing me with an amazing view of her shapely ass and a peek at her intimate flesh. It made me want to go to my knees and taste her. However, we had a game to finish.

She slowly stood up again, the action almost sensual, and stepped over to the soap. I admired her body as she leaned down once more, loving the graceful way she moved. She didn't seem to be aware of it at all, her mind too busy calculating how best to respond to me and this situation.

If she would only look into my eyes, she'd know exactly what I desired.

Alas, she stepped around behind me to clinically soap up my ass. No fondling. No lingering touches. Just Lily performing as she was told out of fear of doing the wrong thing.

Which, by nature, made her actions incorrect.

I caught her wrist as she reached around me to repeat the process with the front.

She was barely touching me, just going through the motions of rubbing soap against my skin. It wasn't anything like the way she'd explored my legs or abs.

"S-sorry," she stuttered.

I faced her, still holding her wrist.

My opposite hand went to her face, my fingers clasping her chin.

"Touch me the way you want to, Lily. Not to please me. But to please yourself. Explore. Stroke. Study me, Lily. Follow your instincts, not your training."

I guided her hand back to my hip and released her wrist.

But I held her chin, wanting to read her emotions through her wide eyes.

Her throat worked as though she wanted to say something.

I waited.

She remained silent.

A sigh caught in my chest, the realization that I would need to end this game hitting me hard in the gut. All I wanted was for her to live a little. However, her fear of failure was holding her captive, making her question every—

Her fingertips twitched, cutting off my thoughts and seizing my focus.

What are you going to do? I asked with my eyes.

She drew her nails across my lower abdomen to the untouched skin below my belly button, the stroke teasingly light.

Then she ever so slowly ventured downward, tracing the thin line of hair down to the base of my shaft. Her pupils pulsated, her tongue slipping out to lick her lips. Then she gradually continued the movement along my length to the head. Just that tender drag of her fingertips.

I allowed her to see the desire in my gaze, the hunger for her to do more. To see how that light touch affected me. To understand how badly I wanted her.

Restraining myself while she explored was no easy feat.

But I did this for her.

A gift.

A way to apologize for confusing her. A way to show my gratitude for her bravery. A way to show how much her existence intrigued me.

I always took charge. However, tonight, I handed her the reins. To an extent, anyway. She needed to experience some control and seek her own enjoyment, to learn how to *live*.

Her fingers wrapped around me, stroking just a little to test the boundaries. I allowed it only because I could scent her own responding arousal.

When I didn't speak or push her away, she grew bolder, her opposite hand joining the other in her exploration. Her cleansing job was much more thorough now, her palms going everywhere and even reaching around to more properly touch my backside.

I forced her to maintain eye contact with me the whole time, demanding that she witness my reactions.

Her cheeks were pink, her breaths came in harsher pants, and her pulse thrummed alluringly. I gave her several minutes, allowing her to do whatever she desired.

Each passing moment heightened the sensual scent in the air, her arousal a beacon that made my mouth water for her.

I wanted to dive between her legs and devour her. Make her scream my name. Listen to her whimpers as I forced her to come again and again against my mouth.

This was the foreplay I craved.

That mindless oblivion that drove women and men to do unspeakable things to each other.

"I'm going to kiss you now, Lily," I whispered, my gaze going to her mouth. "And then I'm going to rinse off."

It would prolong the experience, heighten the illicit

yearning between us, and force her into the mindless state needed for us to succeed in breaking down her walls.

I didn't wait for her acknowledgment or acceptance; I merely claimed her mouth as I stepped backward beneath the massive showerheads. She moved with me, one hand still wrapped around my dick and the other on my ass.

I released her chin to catch the back of her neck, then I deepened our kiss with my tongue.

She moaned, her breasts meeting my chest as she leaned into me. Her grasp around my base tightened, her need a palpable presence between us as the water cascaded over our heads. I captured her ass with my free hand, forcing her even closer.

I wouldn't fuck her.

Not like this.

Not tonight.

But soon.

Very soon.

Just as soon as she understood how pleasure would work between us.

"Games are not always about winning, little flower," I said against her mouth. "Sometimes they are meant for the purpose of mutual enjoyment." And that was the lesson here tonight—that our sensual experiences would entertain both of us, not just me.

Her hand glided along my shaft as her opposite palm slid from my ass to my hip. "I like this game."

I grinned. "I know. I like it, too."

I kissed her again, my grasp against her neck tightening as she applied pressure with her grip below. Then the hand against my hip ventured south to dip between my legs and cup my balls.

"Time for a new game," I told her, breaking our kiss

and grabbing her wrist again. I tugged her out of the shower despite the protest glittering in her gaze.

I wrapped her up in a towel before going back in to flip off the shower.

"Use the towel to dry yourself off. Then go get on the bed," I said without looking at her. "I want you naked with your legs spread and your hands over your head. Understood?"

"Yes, Master Cedric." There wasn't a hint of fear in her tone, only excitement.

But I couldn't stop the growl from leaving my chest as I exited the shower once more. "Cedric, Lily. No *Master*."

She nibbled her bottom lip and considered me for a moment, making me wonder if she wanted to argue the title with me. But she must have decided otherwise because she nodded. "Yes, Cedric."

Well, at least she was being less timid.

I accepted that as a positive start.

"If you really want to please me, you'll spread your legs and bend your knees so I can see that pretty pussy when I walk into my bedroom." I stepped toward her, still damp and naked and painfully hard. "If I like what I see, I'll kiss you properly."

She shivered. "I'm shaved."

"I know. But it's not your bare skin that I want to see, Lily." I leaned in to press my lips to her ear. "I want you excited and begging for my tongue. I want your clit swollen with need. I want that alluring pink flesh so fucking soaked that you leave a wet spot on my bed. I want your natural perfume to choke me like a noose and bring me to my knees."

That last part was already happening, her arousal spiking with each dark comment.

"Go get on the bed, Lily. Show me how you've

blossomed. And if I'm impressed, you'll know by how vigorously I lick you with my tongue."

She quivered so violently that my hands flexed in preparation to catch her.

But she didn't fall. Instead, she dropped the towel and pressed a quick kiss to my cheek before leaving the bathroom.

It was the sexiest invitation I'd ever received—that sweet touch of innocence followed by her shaky walk from the room.

Because those weren't trembles of fear; they were shudders of *need*.

You're almost where I need you, Lily, I thought, picking up the towel she'd dropped. *Tonight, I'm going to make you bloom.*

LILY

Every part of me burned.

My face. My breasts. My lower belly. My thighs.

I fought the urge to squirm, my need for friction driving the heat to uncomfortable levels inside me. My veins resembled liquid fire.

Cedric had sent me in here what felt like hours ago. Except my damp hair told me it was maybe only a few minutes.

Yet it felt as though I were dying.

His words had rippled through me and stoked my inner craving, leaving me more than soaked between my thighs.

I wanted to be embarrassed, but that would require me to have enough energy to feel anything other than aroused, and my emotional reserves were all tapped out at the moment.

I gripped the pillows over my head, my back threatening to bow as a moan taunted my throat.

Goddess, where is he? Why is this taking so long?

I squeezed my eyes shut, a tiny hint of fear taking root inside me.

What if he isn't coming? What if he's just testing me to see how long I'll lie like this, waiting for him?

The answer was forever.

Because I didn't want to be anywhere else. I desired him. And if lying here in a sea of agonizing arousal was what he required, I'd do it.

I swallowed, my skin prickling as my core pulsated with interest.

He'd let me touch him.

His ass. His cock. Every part of him. I'd never experienced such perfection. And the open way he'd let me explore him had only made me burn that much hotter for him.

He'd denied my request to please him. Then he'd demanded that I finish the game properly.

I didn't truly understand his motives, but he'd made it clear that the shower game had been for me. He'd given me the opportunity to explore him on my terms without allowing me to focus on his pleasure.

It was an experience unlike any of my existence.

An experience I would dream about for the rest of my life.

His smooth skin. His hardness. His muscular form. All of it was so perfect that it almost hurt to think about. Mostly because picturing him made me want him, and I was already so *wet*.

"Cedric," I breathed, pained by the need pulsating through my veins. "*Please.*"

I wasn't sure what I truly wanted him to do. Touch me? Lick me? Bite me?

My thighs nearly closed, my desire to rub them together spiking through my mind.

I tightened my hold on the pillows, fighting the urge to touch myself.

So hot.

Where is he? Why isn't he responding? What is this new game?

He wanted me wet and swollen. I couldn't touch my clit, but the way it throbbed suggested it was ready for him.

Dampness trickled down to my ass, again making me want to squirm.

I whispered his name once more, my eyes filling with tears as I began to silently weep for his touch.

I hadn't heard him leave the bathroom. But he could phase. Did he leave me here to suffer? Was this all just another way to break me?

After all the kind things he'd said... was it all a lie?

Is this even real?

My eyes sprang open, my need to verify my surroundings hitting me hard in the chest.

I gasped as I found Master Cedric standing at the foot of the bed. *It's real. He's real. He's* here.

His dark eyes simmered with violent energy, his cheekbones hard enough to cut glass.

He didn't look pleased.

He looked furious.

Are my legs not spread enough apart? I wondered, my thighs automatically trying to stretch more. *Are my heels meant to be closer to my ass?* I tried to slide them farther up the bed, the bend in my legs reminding me of a butterfly's wings by the time I finished.

His expression darkened even more.

I swallowed, my fingers clammy against the pillows.

His anger both unnerved me and... and made me *hotter.*

He was dangerous. Lethal. A predator. And it almost seemed like he wanted to eat me.

Maybe he did.

Maybe he planned to bite me.

Oh, Goddess, that thought just tightened the ache inside me, intensifying my need.

More tears fell, my lips mouthing his name as my back arched off the bed. This was agony, him being so close to my aching flesh. I wanted to scream at him to do something, beg him to take this pain away, demand he touch me.

But I couldn't do those things. Mostly because I didn't know how to properly articulate the desire.

None of my courses had taught me anything about seeking my own pleasure, only how to please males. Specifically, Six. And the classes where he'd practiced on me hadn't been anything like this.

No warmth.

No sensuality.

No extreme sensations of being on the verge of the most beautiful death imaginable.

"Cedric," I said, trying to tell him what I wanted. "I… It *hurts.*"

"I know," he whispered, his hand wrapping around his impressive length to give it a harsh stroke. "You're so fucking wet."

A noise left my mouth that I couldn't define. It sounded almost animalistic, yet borderline desperate.

"Did you please yourself while I was gone?" he asked, his voice still soft as he continued to run his hand up and down his shaft. "Did you think of me when you came?"

My throat was dry, all my moisture seeming to have gone south. "Yes," I admitted. "I thought of you every time."

And the only time I'd really come had been when I'd touched myself.

Six never could bring me to orgasm properly.

Although, I had tried to help a few times by pretending

237

he was Cedric. But it hadn't worked. He wasn't rough enough. Strong enough. *Dominant* enough.

"Put your hand between your legs. Show me how you touch yourself." His voice held a subtle growl to it that had me whimpering.

Or maybe it was his request.

Because I didn't want to touch myself. I wanted him to touch me.

My fists clenched in the pillows rather than obey him. "I want your hand more than mine."

"Are you refusing my request?" he asked, his palm sliding to a halt at his base.

No. That wasn't what I meant. I just… I expected… *him.*

"And if I'm impressed, you'll know by how vigorously I lick you with my tongue."

"Are you not impressed?" I whispered, recalling his heated words from the bathroom. "You said you would tell me with your tongue…" I trailed off, my mind buzzing beneath an avalanche of agonized need. *Please…*

"You just said you want my hand more than your own."

"I do." My ankles were aching from holding this position for him, adding a hint of pain to my voice. But it was worth it if I impressed him enough. "And your tongue," I confessed. "I want you to… to *lick* me."

I'd thought he meant between my thighs.

But maybe I'd misunderstood.

Goddess, I hoped I'd followed correctly. Because it was all I could think about now.

"But you touching yourself would please me, Lily," he cooed. "Are you saying that won't be enough for you? That you need more?"

I bit my lip, the desire to scream hitting me hard. Because yes, I wanted more. I'd just said that!

Another tear fell, the torment leaving me dizzy.

"Do you desire more?" he asked, rephrasing his previous question. "Answer me, Lily. Are you saying you won't please me by putting on a show?"

I started to weep. This was all so wrong. I should be doing everything he wanted. But he'd planted a sensual idea in my head that I couldn't seem to release.

"I want your tongue," I whispered brokenly. "Please, Cedric. I'm swollen, just like you wanted. I'm wet. I'm *hot*. I... I feel like I'm going to explode."

"But that doesn't matter, does it? It's my pleasure that matters most. Isn't that what Master Peyton taught you?"

His words were arrows through my heart.

Because he was right.

This was about him, not me.

Except that wasn't what he'd said in the shower. He wouldn't let me go to my knees then. He'd said that wasn't how the game was played.

So had he done all this to make me mad with lust just to deny me pleasure?

No. He was offering it in the form of my own hand.

I wanted to laugh. Not because it was funny, but because it was just so humiliating and hurtful and *wrong*.

"I hate you," I breathed, my hand releasing the pillow to skate down my body, to do what he'd demanded.

Only, I no longer felt as hot as before.

I felt cold.

But I had to do this for him. It was what he'd demanded, and he was the superior being. The one who issued edicts that I had to follow.

More tears left my eyes as I found my clit, the agony of his new game mixing with the pain of my need.

He caught my wrist, his knee suddenly on the bed as he knelt between my thighs.

"You should hate me," he said, his obsidian irises raging with black fire. "That's our current world. It's cruel. Your desires mean nothing. Your arousal is meant to be a passing enjoyment that's abused and used for someone else's pleasure. Never your own."

I clenched my jaw. "You don't need to remind me of my place. I *know* what I am to you, *Master Cedric*." I circled my clit with my finger to punctuate the point, causing his eyes to lower. "Release me. I'm ready to perform."

He smiled. "That anger you feel right now? *That* is what I desire from you."

"So you tricked me into thinking there would be more just to remind me of my fate, all to provoke anger?" I really did hate this man.

"Yes," he replied. "Because now you're ready to experience it. And you'll appreciate it that much more in the end."

I frowned. "Appreciate what?" I didn't understand a word he was saying.

He crawled over me, his grip on my wrist forcing my hand to move with him. Then he set it back in the pillows beside the other one.

His lips brushed my cheek as he pressed his mouth to my ear. "*My tongue*, Lily."

He nuzzled my jaw, his body not fully touching mine as he balanced his weight on his hands, which he'd placed on the bed on either side of my head.

"Your pleasure doesn't matter to society," he continued, his nose skimming my cheekbone. "Only my pleasure matters, according to your classes. But as I told you in the shower, those courses were not designed with my wants and needs in mind."

I swallowed, his erratic behavior giving me whiplash.

"You're so wet, little flower. You're begging for rapture." His words were almost reverent. "You denied my request and voiced your own. *That* is what I want. *That* is behavior I'll reward."

But he'd just spent the last however many minutes reminding me of my place.

I didn't understand.

Why would he do that? Was this just another trick? A way to mess with me even more?

"Tell me to eat your pussy," Master Cedric said, his mouth hovering over mine. "Demand it and I'll give it to you."

I shuddered. "You're playing with me."

"No, I'm teaching you," he corrected. "You've been taught to only care about the enjoyment of the master you'll serve. But your enjoyment matters to me."

"That's not what you said—"

"I pointed out what the university has taught you. Now I'm instructing you on *my* preferences. So tell me to eat your pussy, Lily. Tell me to lick that sweet little clit until you're crying with pleasure and begging me to stop."

His words stirred the fire inside me, renewing the inferno seeking to destroy my veins.

I hated him for it.

Hated how easily his words provoked such a response.

It was all just a game to him to see if I would follow his orders just so he could humiliate me again.

But a broken part of me wanted to beg.

That shattered part of me wanted to matter, to seek my own pleasure, to make him follow through on his word.

Because I deserved better than this. I didn't want to be a piece of food to be toyed with before a meal.

I wanted more.

I wanted his wicked promises and dark touch.

I wanted the version of Cedric from our shower.

Was he even real?

There was only one way to find out.

To play his game.

He could deny me again. But I would expect it this time. Some new twist.

And that infuriated me.

It made me want to shake him and force his head between my legs, to truly demand that he do something for me for once. Not for him.

I wanted to matter.

I wanted to *feel*.

"Lick me, Cedric," I dared him. "Make me come."

He smiled, and for half a beat, I expected the worst. But he kissed me instead, his tongue mastering mine before he started a delirious path downward.

Licking.

Nibbling.

Nipping me with his teeth.

Never harshly, always teasingly.

Especially against my breasts, where he laved my stiff peaks while holding my gaze.

I nearly came from that attention alone.

But then he continued his sensual trail past my belly button to the damp heat between my thighs.

He didn't tease me there—he *took*. He *claimed*. He *owned*.

His licks were damning, tracing my seam before spearing me deeply. Then he slid his tongue up to my sensitive nub and allowed me to feel his fangs.

I jolted, my heart kick-starting in my chest. *He's going to bite me there.*

I'd seen it done in class before when Master Peyton had

taken a female student aside for punishment. She'd bitten the poor girl while one of the males had fucked the female's mouth.

She'd passed out after minutes of choking noises that sounded like gurgled screams.

The memory of it made me cold, yanking me out of the moment as ice shot down my spine.

Master Cedric's mouth left my center, his fingers replacing his tongue as he slid one inside me and caressed my clit with his thumb.

"I don't know what memory put that haunted look in your eyes, but it has no place here between us," he said softly as he stroked me deep with his finger. "Come back to me, sweet Lily."

A tremble below knocked loose some of the ice building inside me.

Then his mouth sealed around my nipple again, the heat of his tongue a lash against my chilled skin.

He didn't relent, his eyes holding mine as he tormented my breast. Then he switched to the other, and my thoughts melted into the abyss, Master Cedric's mouth my sole focus.

And his fingers.

He'd added a second to my channel below, his thumb still massaging my swollen nub.

I started to pant, the heat singeing my insides all over again and driving me nearly insane.

I needed something more. Something I couldn't convey.

But Master Cedric seemed to know.

Because he moved downward once more, his mouth creating a searing line of open-mouthed kisses all the way down my body.

Until he captured my clit again.

This time with his lips and not his teeth.

He added his tongue, his gaze still holding mine through each instant.

I felt like I was on the verge of death. Shaking. Panting. *Moaning*.

If he stopped now, I'd kill him.

But he seemed intent on finishing this—finishing *me*.

I gave in to it. I let him lead. I granted him access to my very soul. It left me vulnerable in a way I'd never anticipated, but he didn't abuse my trust, his tongue whispering sweet benedictions against my intimate flesh.

The maelstrom inside me continued to build, to roar with need, stoked onward by his tongue, until I felt a temporary paralysis in my limbs that froze me on the very edge of oblivion. It sent a quake through my limbs, my spirit crying out for something I didn't understand.

Until Master Cedric's fang gently skimmed my throbbing flesh, sending me free-falling into a dark insanity.

I screamed, my training nonexistent and incapable of igniting under such duress.

I was lost.

Swimming through a sea of electrifying intensity.

My limbs shook, my stomach clenched, and my heart beat rapidly in my chest.

The climax was so powerful that it hurt.

And Master Cedric wasn't done.

He kept sucking my clit, driving me into another head-on collision with ecstasy that left me shaking beneath him in a delirious state of bliss.

I panted his name, telling him I needed a break.

But he continued, his gaze holding mine as his mouth demanded *more*.

I started to weep, my body telling me I was done.

However, a new storm brewed to life beneath his oral assault, forcing me to accept more, taking me to new heights that threatened to black out my vision.

I nearly begged him to stop.

Just for an explosion to take me to the stars in a new way, leaving me breathless and lifeless on the bed.

Only then did Master Cedric release me, never once having bitten me the way I'd feared.

He even gave my clit a final kiss before going to his knees between my thighs.

I clenched around him, terrified that he intended to fuck me now that I was exhausted from pleasure.

He didn't.

Instead, he pressed his palm to my damp heat, coating his skin with my arousal. Then he wrapped his hand around his shaft and began to stroke, using my slickness as a lubricant.

It was so intense. So hot. So beautiful to watch. He kept his eyes on mine the whole time, his expression darkly hungry.

"I'm going to fuck you," he promised. "Not tonight. But it'll be just like this, after I've driven so much pleasure from you that you think you can't come again. And I'll prove you wrong with my cock."

I shivered, the image his words painted one I rather liked.

"I'm going to take your ass, too. Maybe even the same night. Fill you with my cum and make every part of you mine." His rhythm increased with his words, his muscles flexing in his arm. "You'll taste my cum tonight, Lily. Just like I tasted yours."

I swallowed, already looking forward to his flavor.

"Mmm, you like my plans," he hummed, his pupils pulsating as his grip tightened. "You wanted to please me earlier. Maybe I'll let you tomorrow. But only after I devour you again."

He leaned down to lick me between the thighs, causing me to flinch and moan at the same time.

"So fucking good," he groaned, his expression turning pained. His free hand went to the bed beside me as he leaned over me, the head of his cock brushing my opening as he continued pumping himself. "I'm going to come all over you, Lily. Mark you as mine and make you fly again with my pleasure inside you."

I shuddered, the flames in my veins igniting with excitement despite my tired state.

His head nudged my heat again, making me wonder if he planned to thrust home, but his hand was moving faster now, his pace telling me he was close.

"Grab my shoulders," he commanded.

I obeyed, my fingers loving the feel of his muscular frame.

Then he kissed me as though he required my mouth to breathe.

I responded in kind, losing myself to the sensations brought on by his presence. By his touch. By his tongue. By that intense sensation between his thighs.

I felt close to the edge. My mind catapulting into that delirious state once more.

It was overwhelming insanity.

He wasn't even really stroking me.

Yet I dug my nails into his skin as though I was the one about to explode.

He growled against my mouth, my name a curse on his tongue as his orgasm seized hold of him. Hot ecstasy licked across my flesh, claiming me between my thighs.

"Touch yourself," he demanded. "Rub my cum into your cunt and come again."

I didn't deny his order of self-pleasure this time, my desire to do exactly what he'd said slamming me square in the chest.

Because I wanted his claim.

And just the thought of him releasing his orgasm between my thighs had me on the edge of joining him in sweet oblivion.

My core was soaked with his arousal and mine. I ran my fingers through it and dragged it up to my swollen flesh, rubbing it just like he'd commanded.

It hurt in the best way, my body on the verge of breaking from too much passion.

But I forced myself onward, circling my nub and feeling his intimate claim.

His head nudged my entrance again, driving me that much higher. Then his hand replaced his hardness, his fingers sliding through the mess he'd made and shoving the essence inside me.

"*Ohhh*," I moaned, that possessive action slaying my every thought.

He did it again.

And again.

All the while, I stroked myself.

Until I couldn't think beyond sensation and his presence above me, his lips lingering near mine.

"Come for me," he whispered, his gaze intent. "Right now, Lily. I need to see you fall apart with my cum-drenched fingers inside you."

A violent quake threatened to destroy me.

But I followed it.

Embraced it.

And screamed as it overtook me.

Blackness descended, my world shuddering to an abrupt halt.

Only for Master Cedric's mouth to bring me back to life, his blood a familiar taste against my tongue.

Except his fingers followed, painting my lips in our shared arousal, then he kissed me again, drowning me in the unique flavor of our passion.

I was... done.

Overwhelmed.

Dying.

Yet living for the first time.

All because of his dark games. His mercurial personality. His delirious desires.

"Tomorrow we'll play again," he promised, his lips against my ear. At some point, he'd tucked me against him with my back to his chest. And the residual dampness between my thighs felt fresh and warm, suggesting he'd cleaned me with a wet cloth.

Did I lose consciousness? I wondered dizzily.

"Sleep, my flower," he whispered. "Sleep and we'll indulge each other more tomorrow."

My eyes slid closed.

My world darkening once more.

Except dreams waited for me this time when I slept.

Dreams that quickly morphed into nightmares of Blood Day.

Where the Magistrate was Master Cedric, standing at the podium and sending me to the moon chase with a sadistic smirk on his face.

Run fast, little flower, he whispered. *Run fast until you die.*

Continue reading with *Blood Day: Part II*, the conclusion of the Blood Day duet.

Blood Day Part II

*Once upon a time, humankind ruled the world while lycans and vampires lived in secret.
This is no longer that time.*

Lily

My life is a nightmare.

Every move is controlled by vampires and lycans. Every blink is monitored by the superior beings of my world. Every breath is checked by those who master my kind.

But I've stumbled upon a dream.
A vampire.
A professor at the university whom I should not trust yet can't seem to stop wanting to touch.

Will he be my salvation?
Or will Blood Day destroy us both?

*Welcome to the future where the superior bloodlines make the rules.
You're about to enter the Blood University world, where humans have
no rights. No choices. And there are no second chances.
Proceed at your own risk.*

USA Today Bestselling Author Lexi C. Foss loves to play in dark worlds, especially the ones that bite. She lives in Chapel Hill, North Carolina with her husband and their furry children. When not
writing, she's busy crossing items off her travel bucket list, or chasing eclipses around the globe. She's quirky, consumes way too much coffee, and loves to swim.

Want access to the most up-to-date information for all of Lexi's books? Sign-up for her newsletter here.

Lexi also likes to hang out with readers on Facebook in her exclusive readers group - Join Here.

Where To Find Lexi:
www.LexiCFoss.com

Also by Lexi C. Foss

Blood Alliance Series - Dystopian Paranormal

Chastely Bitten

Royally Bitten

Regally Bitten

Rebel Bitten

Kingly Bitten

Cruelly Bitten

Blood Alliance Standalones - Dystopian Paranormal

Blood Day

Crave Me

Dark Provenance Series - Paranormal Romance

Heiress of Bael (FREE!)

Daughter of Death

Son of Chaos

Paramour of Sin

Princess of Bael

Captive of Hell

Elemental Fae Academy - Reverse Harem

Book One

Book Two

Book Three

Elemental Fae Queen

Winter Fae Queen

Hell Fae - Reverse Harem

Hell Fae Captive

Hell Fae Warden

Immortal Curse Series - Paranormal Romance

Book One: Blood Laws

Book Two: Forbidden Bonds

Book Three: Blood Heart

Book Four: Blood Bonds

Book Five: Angel Bonds

Book Six: Blood Seeker

Book Seven: Wicked Bonds

Book Eight: Blood King

Immortal Curse World - Short Stories & Bonus Fun

Elder Bonds

Blood Burden

Assassin Bonds

Mershano Empire Series - Contemporary Romance

Book One: The Prince's Game

Book Two: The Charmer's Gambit

Book Three: The Rebel's Redemption

Midnight Fae Academy - Reverse Harem

Ella's Masquerade

Crossed Fates

Other Books

Scarlet Mark - Standalone Romantic Suspense

Rotanev - Standalone Poseidon Tale

Carnage Island - Standalone Reverse Harem Romance

Printed in Great Britain
by Amazon

62293697R00160